The Vampire Lucius Lafayette: Volume 2

by

SYLYNT STORME

PUBLISHED BY:
Lemon Tree Publishing

Copyright © 2012 Sylynt Storme

Visit: **http://SylyntStorme.com**

This is a work of fiction. All characters, names, places
and events are the product of the author's
imagination or used fictitiously.

Editing: Dragonfly Editing

ISBN-13: 978-1-927623-17-6

Table of Contents

DEATH'S DOOR

Darina was in her nightie. It was plain cream in color. It wouldn't stay that way for long.

"What have you done?" she asked, rhetorically.

She looked at Lucius and held his face in her hands. She kissed him on the forehead. He coughed up more blood. It was pink and foamy. I think he had been hit in the lungs.

"He took three bullets in the back," I said.

"Help me take off his clothes," she said.

We un-wrapped the red scarf from around his neck. We managed to pull him out of his trench coat and I took off his gloves. Darina tore off his gray turtleneck with her bare hands and we slowly turned him over.

His back was a slippery, red, wet mess. There were two dents in his back about mid-way on his left side. They looked like squashed cherries. On the right side there was another squashed cherry seeping blood. This one was higher up and probably entered his lung.

Darina took her hands and pushed them over his wounds, here and there. She was feeling for the bullets, hoping they were whole. They would be easier to get out that way. Vampires have the ability of telekinesis. Darina was looking away the whole time. Her fingers tapped away on his back as if she were very slowly playing the piano.

"Good," she said, "good."

"What's good?" I asked. Lucius had lost consciousness. That didn't look good to me.

"The bullets are intact," she said. "That's very good."

She wasn't looking at me. She was still looking away, down the hall at the main entrance door. Almost expecting someone to come in. Her fingers still pushed and probed. Softly. She wasn't trying to extract the bullets with her fingers. That's not how telekinesis works. Her fingers and hands moved over his back, slowly, earnestly.

I watched in awe. She was smudging his seeping blood all over his back like it was a canvas and she was creating an abstract. She was oblivious to all of this. Then she took her left hand away, and a squashed slug, like a gray cherry stone appeared in her hand. She put in down next to us on the floor. A few moments later another one came out and she put it next to the first one. I saw this one come out of his body. Almost coaxed, how you might squeeze an orange pip from an orange segment.

With those two out, it left the last one. The one that I imagined was embedded in his lungs.

"This one is more difficult," she said talking down the hallway. "Help me, please. Keep him steady."

Lucius was coming to. He was groaning and squirming. I placed my hands on his shoulders and tried to steady him.

"Better," she said. "Hold him steady. I don't want the bullet to cause any more tearing of the lung membranes as it comes out."

She was using both her hands over his right upper back, just below the shoulder. Her hands looked like spiders dancing on his back. They were dipped in red. His blood was everywhere. It was seeping onto the floor and creating a small puddle. Finally, the bullet came out.

"Help me take him upstairs," she said.

We carried him up into the main bedroom and placed him on his stomach. The white sheets were clean. Recently changed.

"That's not important!" she said, snapping at me. "Can't you see he's dying?"

"Sorry," I said and smiled weakly, like thin tea.

Darina kneeled next to him and slashed her right wrist open with her finger. Blood started pouring out and she fed it into the wounds. I couldn't tell if her blood was going in or his blood was coming out. There was just a shimmering wet mirror of blood all over his back.

After she had given him as much blood as she could manage, she took each of the entrance wounds and squeezed them tight, sealing them. Lucius moaned and twitched. It looked painful.

"Go get Ezra," she said to me.

"Where is he?" I asked.

"Down in the French Quarter, feeding," she said.

She closed her eyes and focused in on him.

"1024 Chartres Street. The Hotel Provincial, Room 209."

I left her there, sitting next to Lucius. He had lost consciousness again when I left. When I arrived at the hotel, I quickly climbed the stairs to the second level and made my way to room 209. The door was closed. I tried it. It opened.

Inside was a mess. Three gangsters were crumpled like bad origami on the floor. They were peppered with bullet holes. Up on the bed, against the wall, Ezra was quenching on a black woman. Her upper body was naked and her breasts hung like the jowls of a bloodhound. Ezra was holding her up by the throat with his right hand. She looked like she was sleeping. He was quenching on the right side of her neck. Her toes were barely touching the white pillows. All she had on was a red thong.

Ezra looked at me without taking his mouth from his victim. In his left hand I saw his Glock 20 hanging loosely like it was a wilted flower. He raised his eyebrows at me.

"It's Lucius," I said.

He pulled away from the black woman. Her complexion looked more ashen than a warm brown. He was practically finished with her. He still held her up against the wall, her feet still dangling.

"What?" he said.

"Lucius has been shot," I said. "You need to get back home quickly."

He dropped the semi-naked women like a sack of flour. Before she lay quiet and dead on the bed, Ezra was in front of me.

"Well then, let's go," he said.

He grabbed me, and we apotrepinated. We arrived in the living room in a swirl of coal black smoke. Ezra was resting his hands on his knees.

"God, that's too far to do that too often," he said, between gasps of breath. His left hand was holding the Glock and it was pointed at my shoes.

"Do you mind?" I said pointing at the barrel of the gun.

He looked down at it. His finger was around the trigger.

"Right, sorry."

He put it away under his right arm, in its holster.

"He's upstairs," I said.

We left the living room and Ezra took the flight of stairs in one leap. I was right behind him, as best as I could.

Darina looked around at us as we arrived in the room.

"Thanks for coming, darling," she said to Ezra.

"Jesus," he said, "what happened?"

Darina looked at me, like it was my fault. Like I might have been the one pulling the trigger. Ezra looked at me too, more curious than anything.

"We were hunting vermin in Queens in 1977," I said. "Lucius was after Son of Sam, or more accurately, the satanic cult that Son of Sam was involved with at the time, called the Hell's Disciples."

I stopped and looked over at Lucius. Other than the blood slowly caking on his back, he looked as peaceful as a baby.

"Go on," said Ezra.

"Anyway, I told him that he should have brought you along, but he said he couldn't find you. There were a lot of them and we figured out that they were part of the Galletti pack from old Italy."

Ezra shook his head and cursed under his breath.

"I know," I said. "Anyway, we arrived just after the Freund and Diel shooting. There were a bunch of them and Lucius started off strong. Son of Sam bolted when he saw what Lucius was up to. But the shooter stayed behind and Lucius had forgotten about her. She shot him three times in the back."

"And you were just standing around watching?" asked Darina.

It was another rhetorical question that I chose not to answer.

"Mom," said Ezra, "let's focus on dad here."

He went up to his father and brushed his hair away.

"He's not doing well. He needs more vampire blood."

"I know," she said, "but we can't get him to quench or drink. We need a transfusion. Who's the closest vampire doctus?"

Ezra thought for a moment.

"I think that's Doctus Emilio of the San Antonio Davidyan Killing."

"Go and get him. Hurry, and then go and get your brother."

Ezra grabbed me, and we headed down stairs just as Genevieve came home from a play. She sensed something was wrong as soon as she saw the big smudge of burgundy on the wooden floor of the foyer.

"He's upstairs," Ezra said, "go and comfort mother. I'm going to get the doctus."

Genevieve ran up the stairs as Ezra opened up a TimeDent. He dialed in San Antonio and we arrived on East Contour Drive, just outside a large million dollar estate home that was owned by the Davidyan Killing. We walked up the long drive between immaculate lawns and old trees. Trees, some of which had been around since the Battle of the Alamo.

Ezra knocked on the door with the door knocker. It was a large brass ring held between the teeth of the lion. An older gentleman with sad, watery eyes opened up the door.

"Baron Lafayette," he said. "What a pleasure."

"We need the doctus," said Ezra as the butler opened the door and let us in.

He wandered off down the hall and disappeared down a corridor and into a side room. He reappeared a moment later with a tall skeleton of a man. This was Doctus Emilio. He was as old as time itself, and he looked it. In his hand he held a large black doctor's bag that looked like it was a couple of hundred years old. The black leather was now an elephant gray, and it looked as worn. On the top were the initials EK in inch large gold letters.

His head was bald, his lips thin and his gait somewhat hunched, but he was the best vampire doctus on the continent. He smiled warmly as he saw Ezra, and you couldn't help but feel calmed in his presence.

"Baron Ezra," he said, shaking his hand. "How may I help?"

"It's my father, Lucius," said Ezra, and I thought I heard a slight crack in his voice, like a hardboiled egg being tapped. "He's been shot and he's not doing well."

"Sorry to hear that," he said. "Give me a moment to collect my things."

He left and disappeared into the room he had come from. Ezra paced the floor back and forth, biting his lip, his head down and his forehead furrowed. The butler stood with his hands behind his back, unsure what to do.

"Please give our regards to Vrykolakas Zedock Davidyan," I said smiling at the butler. "Hopefully, next time we might have a chance to visit."

Ezra nodded his head, not looking up from his pacing.

"Very good, sir," he said and disappeared again, off into the kitchen I imagined.

Doctus Emilio came back out and walked up to us. He was carrying his bag again and it seemed heavier. It was bulging.

"After you, Baron," he said to Ezra.

Ezra looked up at him, confused for just a moment.

"Yes, right," he said.

He opened up a TimeDent and we stepped into it. This time we arrived at the top of the stair landing. Ezra made his way down the hall and then turned into his parent's bedroom. Doctus Emilio and I followed after. Emilio put his bag on the side table. He looked down at Lucius. Lucius was pale, looking like one of those feeble, mythical vampires that humans are always writing about. His eyes swam under his heavy lids. His back was clean, hardly any sign of the bullet wounds. Only small mounds of flesh, like boils, indicated where they were.

Emilio put his fingers to Lucius' neck and looked at his watch, counting. He then put his stethoscope on Lucius' back. Listened for a while. Then moved the stethoscope and listened again. He did this two more times.

"Ta, ta," he said, shaking his head. "This is not good."

He took his fingers and gently placed them on the bubbles of skin which had sealed over the bullet holes. He pushed them. They were soft and squishy like blisters.

"Who did this?" he asked, frustration in his voice.

"I did," said Darina, "I didn't want him to keep bleeding out."

Emilio shook his head.

"Ta, ta," he said again. "His blood will poison him if it can't release the toxins. This is no good. You should not have done this."

With his fingernail he slit each of the wounds. A clot limped out, followed by a trickle of blood from each of the wounds. Darina put her hand to her mouth and started to sob.

"What have I done," she whispered to herself.

Emilio looked at her and patted her shoulder.

"It is okay," he said, "you'll know for next time. All is not lost. But in grievous injuries like this the idea, while sounding counterintuitive, is to allow the vampire to bleed out, within reason, so that the poisons from the lead and other metals created when in contact with his blood can escape. Once that is accomplished, and with a vampire transfusion, we should expect the Baron to fully recover."

Darina blotted her eyes.

"Thank you, Doctus," she said.

He smiled at her, and you immediately felt the calmness of his presence.

"Now, please help me lay him out at about shoulder height so we can allow for the collection of his blood and start the transfusion."

Telekinetically they lifted Lucius off the bed and suspended him about three feet above it. Emilio folded Lucius' arms over his stomach and placed three pewter colored metal cups about four inches under each of his wounds. These cups were about eight ounces in size with a coarse finish inside and out, like sandpaper. They were also suspended in the air telekinetically.

The doctus saw me looking at them with a quizzical look on my face.

"These chalices will help filter the impurities from his blood so that we might transfuse it back into him when pure."

I nodded.

"Can I do anything to help?" asked Genevieve.

"Yes," he said, "you can suspend these transfusion bags about three feet above your father, just off to the side."

Emilio reached into his bag and pulled out four large plastic bags filled with burgundy colored blood. They were each the size of ten pound flour bags. They were heavy. I could see the muscles like thick cables twitch in his forearm as he pulled each one out.

Genevieve, with Ezra's help, suspended them above her father like Emilio had requested.

"Doctus," says Genevieve, "is this not too much blood for my father?"

"I hope so, though I have used this much before, and thankfully, the patient survived. We are dealing with terrible injuries, not the least of which is the poisoned blood. Your father's body will try and expel all this poisoned blood if it can, so we must be ready."

The pewter chalices underneath Lucius were filling up. Emilio changed them out with new ones and placed the full ones on the side table. They looked like goblets full of a thick, robust merlot.

"Please," said Genevieve to me, "that's my father you're talking about."

"Well, I bet it'd be just as tasty," I said, trying to add levity to the gloomy mood. Lucius would have appreciated it.

"Yes, he would," said Ezra smiling.

Emilio took some rubber tubing from his bag. He squeezed the one end and what looked like a vampire's fang erupted from it. He pushed this into one bag of blood. He squeezed the other end and another vampire-looking fang popped out the end. He thrust this into Lucius' neck. Slowly the blood snaked its way through the tube before disappearing into Lucius' neck.

Emilio reached into his bag and pulled out what looked like an eight inch wizard's wand. It was of a similar metal to the chalices. It had a smooth, finely polished, two inch handle and the rest was a knobby, sandpapery looking finish. He dipped it into each of the three chalices and stirred them each a few times. The blood changed color, looking like mercury for a few seconds, and then it changed back to a brighter, redder burgundy. At the same time the chalices turned black.

"Good," said Emilio, watching.

He took each of the chalices, sliced open a slit in the transfusion bag and poured the now clean blood into the bag. He shook them each vigorously after emptying them and they changed back to pewter.

It was time to change the chalices again. The ones under Lucius were filling up and the whole procedure was done again. By the time the second group of three chalices had cleaned the blood and Emilio had poured them back into the transfusion bag, the bag was half empty.

"Excellent," said Emilio.

"Is this good?" asked Darina.

Emilio nodded his head and smiled broadly.

"Baron Lucius has tremendous healing powers. I have never seen such a short recovery. I doubt we will need to use more than two bags of Davidyan blood."

To us, it looked like Lucius was bleeding to death.

"Speak for yourself," said Genevieve to me.

Well, he didn't look like he was healing. His blood was still dripping out of his wounds consistently and his complexion still looked pale. To me he didn't look much better than when we arrived back home about an hour ago.

"Ah, yes," said Doctus Emilio to me, "but you do not have the trained eye. I have been doing this since Christ was on the cross, and mark my words, he is healing extraordinarily quickly and well. I doubt you will need me much longer than sun up."

"Thank you, Doctus," said Darina, "we are very grateful for your help."

He shook his head.

"It is nothing. This is what I do."

The chalices were changed as was the transfusion bag. Lucius was on his second transfusion of Davidyan blood. He was improving, slowly. You could see his tone coming back, although he was still sleeping.

Downstairs the door opened. Nobody noticed.

"We did notice," said Ezra, "we're just focusing on our father."

Okay, the door opened but nobody paid any attention to it. Creaking footsteps could be heard on the landing leading upstairs. We turned to look as Cage came in. He was dressed all in leather. Leather bike pants and a leather jacket. His motorcycle gloves were stuck in his back pockets like tissues. His eyes were hard and his brown hair was an unruly mess, like a badly built nest.

Darina turned and smiled at her youngest son. Ezra looked over at him and smiled briefly before he turned serious. We could all smell the liquor on Cage's breath.

"I'm so glad you've come home, honey," said Darina. "Your father was at death's door, but he is slowly recovering now. I'm sure he'll be very happy to hear that you've come home."

Cage didn't say anything. He stood by the door, his hands down by his side.

"I didn't come home to pay my respects. I've come home to take my rightful place as the head of the Lafayette Killing."

He was looking past his father and out through the windows.

"Stop kidding around," said Ezra, "and stop drinking so damn much. It does you no good."

Cage looked at his brother and smirked.

"It does me well, brother. And I am here to put an end to father's reign of tyranny."

"No, you're not. I am the first born and I will inherit the Killing," said Ezra.

"Cage, stop talking crazy," said Genevieve. "Why don't we go get you some hot chocolate from downstairs?"

Genevieve walked over and tried to take Cage by the elbow, but he shrugged her off. He flew at his father, but Ezra caught him in midair. Cage's hand grazed past Lucius' ribs, slicing him open superficially. Emilio and Darina were caught off guard and everything came tumbling down. The chalices, the blood bag and Lucius on top of it all.

The chalices banged against the soft mattress and spilt tongues of blood like red wine over the white sheets. Lucius, deeply asleep, bounced once then twice on the mattress before lying still. The blood bag was still attached to his neck, but the slit that Emilio had created in it was starting to leak blood.

Ezra flew his brother against the wall where they both crashed hard into it. Cage threw him off and flew for his father again. He landed on top of him, straddling him with his hand above his head, ready to slash down at his father's neck. Just as he did so, Ezra caught him, and Cage's hand grazed across Lucius' cheek, cutting it open to the gums.

They tumbled on the floor flying and jumping each other across the room and into the ceiling and back down to the ground. Ezra finally cornered Cage against the wall, holding him by the throat.

"Enough!" he said.

Cage kneed Ezra in the groin and Ezra buckled, relaxing his grip. Cage went for his father again. This time Genevieve caught him and they tumbled off the bed. Cage threw Genevieve off him and she tumbled and slid out the door, banging against the wall across the hall. Cage got up and looked like he was going for his father one more time.

I heard four gunshots, and saw four bullets graze Cage, one on each side of his face and two between his legs.

"The next one is in your heart," said Ezra. He blinked a tear from his eye. "Don't make me do this."

Cage looked at his older brother. He was breathing hard. His face was an ugly mess of hatred and his brown eyes were as cold as frozen shit. His lungs bellowed, and the veins on the side of his neck bulged like tension wires.

"Don't," said Ezra again. "I love you, Brother, but I will do it."

Another tear leaked out of his eye. Cage looked at him. Darina moved into the line of fire with her back to Ezra.

"Leave, Cage, and don't ever come back until you are sincerely sorry for what you have done here tonight."

In a puff of black inky smoke, Cage apotrepinated out of the room. A moment later we heard his motorcycle snort to life and he squealed out of the driveway and down the road.

Darina and Ezra suspended their father back above the bed, along with the chalices and blood bag.

"How is he, Doctus?" asked Darina.

"He is okay. This hasn't helped, but it hasn't hurt much either."

Emilio took his fingers and sealed the wound across Lucius' cheek. The blood bag was two thirds full and the chalices were once again slowly filling up.

"There is no point crying over spilled blood," said Emilio trying for some levity.

All through the night we held vigil over Lucius' recovering body. He barely stirred. Before the morning sun could poke its ginger head above the horizon Emilio had finished transfusing the third Davidyan blood bag. By this time, the three gunshot wounds on Lucius' back had stopped dripping blood and were slowly starting to heal.

Doctus Emilio was packing away all his tools in his bag. Just before he was done he pulled out a large bulb of garlic. It was the size of an orange. Its papery skin was silver.

"We have been cultivating this Vampyri garlix for centuries now. It will help speed his recovery," said Emilio.

Darina, Ezra and Genevieve stared at this ancient plant from their home. Something they had never seen but only heard their father talk about.

Emilio pulled out an ancient coin, bright, polished silver in color, with Vampyri writing on it. It almost fit in the palm of his hand. He pulled out another smaller bag of blood we hadn't seen before. This carried about eighteen ounces of blood. It was also clear. He put a small slit in the top and dropped the silver coin inside the bag. Then he sealed the bag again.

"That is an ancient Vampyri Vascin. The old coins we used to use for currency. It is pure Vampyri silver. More powerful than Earth's silver. It will purify this blood and energize it," said Emilio. "Let it sit in this blood until you have used it all. Then keep it for additional use when you have the need. I want you to take one garlix clove and three ounces of this Davidyan blood and blend them together. Let Lucius quench on this three times a day for three days and he will be right as rain in no time."

Vampire blood is the most potent blood needed for a vampire to heal. Thin and weak human blood would not have worked to help Lucius survive. And werewolf blood, although powerful, requires a healthy vampire to utilize for sustenance.

"Thank you so much, Doctus," said Darina. "We owe Vrykolakas Zedock a large debt."

Emilio smiled.

"It is nothing," he said. "We are happy to help, as we know you would help in return."

Darina nodded. He kissed her on both cheeks; he kissed Ezra and Genevieve on both cheeks. This is what vampires do. It was a sign of respect. A non-threatening gesture to bring your mouth close to another vampire's throat. Similar to how we shake hands.

They all walked out and down the stairs into the main foyer. Doctus Emilio apotrepinated out.

"Thank God for Vampyri Doctus," said Ezra.

Genevieve smiled and nodded. Darina smiled weakly, looking down at the mess that still needed to be cleaned.

"I'll take care of that, mother," said Genevieve.

"You and I," said Ezra to me, "are going to exact some revenge for this madness."

Darina touched him on the forearm.

"Don't honey, there has been enough bloodshed already tonight."

"No, mother, not quite enough yet."

Ezra walked back up the stairs and into his room. I followed him. He put on a black metallic arm band that looked very similar to a human watch. It was, in fact, a super computer; that is the closest in human terms to explain it. But it is much more than that. The Vampyri call it a voltaren.

"We need to find out just where that human bitch went. Or where she is now," he said.

He tapped a few times on the face of the voltaren and rotated the dial. In front of us a large holographic screen came up.

"You know what would help?" he said.

I shrugged.

"A piece of that wench."

He left his room, went back down stairs and returned moments later holding the three squashed leaden bullets. He tapped on the screen in front of us and brought up a small holographic bowl. He placed the bullets in it. When the voltaren was finished it incinerated the bullets right in front of us. They disappeared in a small puff of grey smoke.

Several images came up before us. They zoomed in on people and where they were. The first was of Lucius. That's not what Ezra wanted so he tossed it aside. Another was of a gun store owner, that's also not what he wanted. These were all the people who had left small bits of their DNA associated with these bullets.

The fifth image that came up was a bingo. It was of a woman loading the bullets into that gun. Ezra spun a dial on the screen and images of her whirred by fast, with dates. He stopped it at December 31, 1999.

This woman, her name came up just above her and followed her around on the screen, was Alma Ivie, with a DOB of February 6, 1947. She was out at Times Square with her husband, we presume, and two other young adults. Perhaps her children. They were watching the New Year's Eve celebrations.

Ezra tapped at the screen some more and a blue flashing icon appeared over a map and zoomed us in to a building on Taylor Avenue in the Bronx. The address read 309 1435 Taylor Avenue. Ezra tapped on the screen and the building opened up and we flew inside it like a bird.

The Vampyri technology is incredible. We were soon inside 309. It was a shit hole with two bedrooms, messy plates piled in the sink and to the side. Newspapers were strewn across coffee tables and kitchen room tables. Ashtrays piled high with ash and crippled cigarette butts. Two bedrooms and a bathroom. The bathroom was filthy. You wouldn't allow werewolves to bathe in it.

"Good," Ezra said, "very good."

He spun the dial more slowly, it turned over onto January 1, 2000. At around two thirty-three in the morning, Alma Ivie and her clan were walking back into their building.

"We know what we need to do," said Ezra.

He rotated the dial on the voltaren, tapped on some buttons and the screen disappeared. He took it off and put in a drawer. Out of that same draw, he pulled out two more magazines for his Glock. He put a fresh one in it and put the other one in his pocket.

"Let's go," he said.

He opened up a TimeDent and we stepped into it. We walked out the other side into 309 1435 Taylor Avenue. It was as dingy as it had looked earlier. We were in the living room. It was dark except for light coming in through the windows from the street lamps. Ezra walked over to a cushy recliner in the corner of the living room. He turned on a floor lamp. It spilled yellow light into the room, making it look even worse.

The walls needed cleaning. The carpet was stained and had several cigarette burns pockmarked over its face. The recliner was draped with a loosely knit blanket. Ezra walked into the main bedroom and turned on the light, it was also a mess. The dresser was strewn with knick knacks and a thin layer of dust. So was the night stand. Ezra opened up drawers with his gloved hands but didn't find any weapons. He opened the closet. Clothes were hanging on hangers at awkward and precarious angles. Clothes were also piled up on the floor of the closet. Dirty ones, presumably.

He left the main bedroom, turning off the light, and checked out the other bedroom. Hard to differentiate the two.

We came back out and he sat down on the recliner. The springs were uneven and it made the chair uncomfortable.

"Ain't that the truth," he said to me.

"Watch the door," he said and I stepped up next to it, so it would swing towards me and hide me from those entering.

Ezra was facing the door at a forty-five degree angle. On his right was a small bookshelf with some books leaning and lying flat. Some had jumped to their deaths on the floor. He picked up a leather bound King James Bible. All it said on the front was "Holy Bible" and it had a line underneath it.

"I love this book," he said to me, "full of such good violence and hyperbole. These humans, even two thousand years ago, had such vivid imaginations."

I looked at my watch it was two twenty nine.

"Four minutes," I said to him.

"Super," he said.

He started to browse the bible, turning the pages with his left hand which also held the Glock. The Glock's barrel swept a frown in front of him as he turned each page. We could hear water trickling and banging in the pipes of this building. We could hear the thumping of music drift by from cars driving past outside. We also heard chatter and loud talking in the halls, now and then.

Then we heard Alma Ivie and her crew walking down the corridor towards us. They weren't saying much.

"So much for Y2K," said Alma, "I guess we gonna have to get a computer now."

"Ain't that the truth," said an older male's voice.

Keys jangled and somebody fumbled with them, missing the lock a couple of times, before getting it in.

"You need more to drink," said the same male voice.

"Fuck you, I don't," she said.

The door swung open and everybody walked in. The young woman closed it behind them and as she saw me she gasped.

"What the fuck!"

"Settle down, now," said Ezra. "That's no language for a lady."

They all looked towards Ezra and his Glock, with its muzzle pointing at them. Four jaws slackened and fell open as if they were hoping for flies. Funnily, despite the mess in here, there were no flies. Maybe because it was winter.

"Who the fuck are you?" yelled the older man. His voice was cracked and chipped and the fear strangled his throat even as he tried to sound tough.

"Shh," said Ezra putting the Glock to his lips as if it were his finger. "Sit down and all will be revealed to you."

He pointed towards the couch with the gun. It was a two seater but it was amazing how accommodating it was for the four of them. Squished together, shoulder to shoulder, sitting board straight.

The younger woman was starting to cry.

"What you gonna do to us, Mister," she said.

"I'm going to kill," said Ezra. I rolled my eyes.

"What?" he said to me.

"That's not how you calm people down."

The younger woman started crying louder. Alma yelled.

"Help, help!" she said.

Ezra looked at her.

"Be quite," he said.

She didn't. So he shot her in the knee. She started sobbing and crying in pain. She dropped to the floor in front of the couch, writhing theatrically.

"Tell your mother to behave," said Ezra.

"Mom, please, please, be quiet."

After a few moments Alma settled down, wincing and moaning every so often.

"So, you folks are wondering why you're here. Besides it being your apartment," said Ezra.

"Listen, Mister," said the younger guy, "you're not gonna get away with this, you hear."

"Quiet," said Ezra, looking down the barrel and pointing the Glock at the young man. He quieted down.

"I want to read you a bit from this lovely novel I have here. You guys call it the King James Bible. I call it a fairytale."

He turned the pages until he found what he was looking for.

"This little ditty is from Deuteronomy, chapter five, verse nine. You shall not bow down yourself to them, nor serve them: for I the LORD your God am a jealous God, visiting the iniquity of the fathers on the children to the third and fourth generation of them that hate me."

They stared blankly at him, blinking, trying to collect flies into their mouths.

"God damn, these sheeple don't have a clue what this means." He was talking to me.

"I am your God," he said to them, pointing the Glock at himself. "And I am jealous of your betrayal. Because of that, I am going to punish the sins of the fathers upon the sons and their sons. But in this case, I am going to punish you all for the sins of your mother... or spouse."

He said that last part for the benefit of the husband.

"You see," Ezra continued, "your mother here," and he pointed at her with the gun, "tried to kill my father around twenty two years ago. Do you remember that?"

She shook her head but didn't look at him.

"Don't fucking lie to me or I'll shoot you right now. It was the summer of seventy-seven."

She nodded.

"You were hanging around with a gang called the Hell's Disciples. A gang of werewolves."

She nodded again.

"Son of Sam was part of your group, and damn if I'm not disappointed that you're not a werewolf. I prefer killing werewolves."

"Listen, I'm sorry. I didn't know he was your father. I was just tryin' to protect myself, see."

"Bullshit. You shot him in the back in cold blood."

Ezra's bright blue eyes were turning a steely gray. That was never a good sign. He was heading off the reservation.

"And you," Ezra said, looking at the older man, "you, robbing little old ladies when you're making deliveries to them. That's vile."

"You don't understand, we need the money. They don't mind."

He grinned sheepishly and shrugged, trying to offer a guilty plea.

"And nothing good can come from the spawn of these two," said Ezra waving the Glock from Alma to her husband.

"You are what are called the sins of the mother, and must be eradicated."

"No, please," sniveled the young woman. "Please don't, we'll be good. We'll behave. I promise, Mister."

"That too, is unbecoming of a lady," said Ezra and he shot her between the eyes. She fell back against the couch, a dribble of blood seeped out the front of her forehead like an exclamation mark.

"I am Vampyri and you do not cross me."

He shot the young man next, right in the same place as his sister. Then he shot the husband through the mouth, as he desperately tried to plead for his life.

"Do you have anything you'd like to say to me?" he asked Alma.

Alma tried to get up to a sitting position, but her bum knee wouldn't let her. She propped herself up against the edge of the couch. Tears were streaming from her eyes. She clutched her two hands in front of her in supplication.

"I'm sorry, Mister, I'm really sorry. I been better lately. I'm trying," she said.

"No, you haven't. You're still filthy trash trying to get the better of others."

She opened her mouth to beg again and he shot her through the eye and then he shot her through the other eye. She looked like a doll as she slumped to the side and lay there. A doll without eyes. Blood trickled out of her sockets and stained the floor. Ezra looked at me.

"I think our work here is done."

CAGED HEART

The days seemed to drag along, taking their time like old, crippled men crossing crosswalks. Darina and Genevieve, especially, were concerned, sitting on pins and needles waiting for Lucius to fully recover.

On the second day after the shooting Lucius actually got up out of bed. Much to Darina's protestations. He insisted though, that he was feeling much better, and as such, needed to get out of bed and stretch his legs a bit, as he said. I was delighted about it. I thought it was about time he got up and about. I had been bored pottering around the house all day, bored and looking for things to do.

Nobody had heard from Cage since the incident where he tried to murder his father. That was an act that I feared would not go unpunished. The only problem was that the Lafayette Killing only had three males, if you count Cage. There was enough strenuous work for three vampires keeping the lid on the Lobison, but likely too much work for two.

Vampyri may be practically immortal but that doesn't mean they are immortal. Nor does it suggest that they don't tire from all the ongoing killing. Not tire in a mental or emotional sense, but just physically tire. And as you can see, if a vampire is not smart with how they conduct themselves, they'll end up injured. Or worse, God forbid, dead.

It was the fourth day after the shooting when I saw Lucius come down for breakfast. I had brewed a big pot of coffee hoping for as much. I was all grins and smiles. A veritable toothpaste commercial. Only he and I were downstairs early in the morning. I was restless, I wanted some action and I was hoping he'd be up for some soon.

"You had us all worried there," I said to him.

He didn't look at me for a moment. He yawned and poured himself a large cup of coffee. He put sugar in it, stirred it more than it needed, then came and sat down in the chair across from me. He was wearing his red satin bathrobe.

He put his hand on my shoulder and looked into my eyes with his intense blue eyes.

"You're a good companion," he said, "taking care of me back then and getting me back here safe."

"Well, you got yourself back, I just helped," I added. Which, in reality, was the truth.

"I appreciate it, nonetheless."

We sat in silence for a while, watching the purple, bruised morning sky heal into the bright blue of full day. After some time, Darina came down and joined us. She helped herself to some coffee, cream and sugar for her. It was the second pot I had brewed. She kissed Lucius on the cheek and sat down next to him. She had bags under her eyes, not having slept well for a while. Worried sick.

"How are you feeling, love?" she asked him.

"Terrific," he said. "Ready to kill some more Lobison."

"I think you should be taking a rest from that for a while. You've given me a few scares the last few weeks. Twice we almost lost you, in fact."

She held his hand and turned towards him. Looking searchingly and sincerely in his eyes.

"I know," he said, "but that was mostly my own undoing. I should never have been so foolish as to turn my back on some werewolves. That was my own fault; I should be more careful next time."

"Maybe you should think about retiring," she said. "I mean, you aren't getting any younger."

This was true. Lucius was over 3,300 years old. Certainly middle aged, at least, for a vampire.

"God, you guys make it sound so old. I feel fine. In fact, I've never felt better as a werewolf slayer. And moreover, who will go on taking care of our vermin problem with these rabid dogs?"

He sipped his coffee and looked across the kitchen table into the dark recesses of his own mind.

"I think it is a younger man's game. You and I could head on over to Orleans and speak with the Council of Vampyri and ask for a change of scenery. Perhaps we could head back home. I think you've earned a rest, at least. They can find another Vrykolakas for New Orleans."

Lucius didn't say anything to that. He was still staring away. His hands curled around his coffee cup and steam snaked up from the hot beverage like fragile thoughts. He slowly shook his head.

"No," he said, "that won't do. I enjoy cleaning up the stench of rabid dogs from this planet too much to give it up yet."

He turned towards Darina and took her hand in his and he looked her in the eyes.

"You've been a patient woman and a good partner to me all these years. But you know that I am a werewolf killer. I have been since before I could apotrepinate. I've loathed them with my whole being. I am lost if I am not hunting them down and putting them out of our misery."

"But, you've been doing it for so long. Surely you must be getting tired of it by now?" she asked.

Again he shook his head, and his bright blue eyes searched hers.

"No, not yet. I am sure there will come a time when I do tire of it. But that time is not now. The time now is for killing more werewolves. You know how quickly and easily they reproduce. Like scum. Our work is seldom done. I cannot rest until I've driven the very last of them out of New Orleans. At the very least."

He patted the hand he held with his other hand.

"It is the very least I can do. When our sector is the cleanest on this planet, then, and perhaps only then, will I feel comfortable enough in resting."

Darina looked down, not liking what she heard. Though he was right about one thing. She had known him as a werewolf slayer all the many hundreds of years they had been together. But he was either getting slow or too comfortable. She had never seen him this close to death before. He seemed to be losing his edge.

Lucius looked to me and his blue eyes smoldered and burned at me.

"I have not lost my edge. I have made some errors. That is all."

"Fine," I said, "but your wife has a point and you need to think about all of us. We can't afford you to be reckless."

Genevieve came down stairs and joined us. She took a cup of coffee and kissed her father on the forehead.

"How are you feeling, Daddy?" she asked.

"Much better now," he said, smiling at her. The apple of his eye.

"Good," she said, "I was so worried by it. You gave me such a fright. I thought you might die."

And her eyes misted up. Lucius took her hands in his and kissed the backs of them, one at a time.

"I made some bad errors in judgment. Your mother, too, got quite the shock. It won't happen again. I promise."

And he looked up at her and gazed at her steadily. She looked at him. Then after a while she looked back down, taking her hands from his and placing them in her lap. She nodded.

"Okay, Daddy," she said. "I hope so."

And we sat in silence for a while.

"Do we have any more of that Davidyan blood?" he asked.

"No," replied Darina shaking her head.

"That's a shame. It was very robust. Really helped me heal much faster than I might otherwise have healed."

"We can always get Ezra to head back out to San Antonio and ask for more blood from the Davidyan Killing, I'm sure they would be more than happy to give us some more," said Darina.

Lucius shook his head.

"No, that won't be necessary," he said, "but I think I'll need a quenching today to keep my strength up."

Ezra came down stairs to join the rest of his family. His hair was an unruly mess of black curls. He yawned and rubbed his eyes and said good morning to everyone.

"Glad to see you up and about, Father. Are you feeling better?" he asked.

"Tip top," said Lucius.

Ezra nodded and sat down at the table with the rest of us. He had drained the last bit of coffee from the coffee pot. He stared into his mug for a bit, a thoughtful expression on his face. Then he frowned.

"What are you going to do about Cage?" he asked into his coffee cup.

Darina frowned at him as if to quiet him. He wasn't looking at her.

"What do you mean?" asked Lucius.

"Nothing, Daddy, he doesn't mean anything," said Genevieve.

"He does mean something, Gen, no need trying to protect your brother. I know what happened."

Ezra looked up at his father and looked him in the eyes.

"Well, if you know, then what are you going to do?" he asked again.

Lucius finished his coffee and put it on the table in front of him. He clasped his hands together, resting them on the tabletop. He was looking over at me but not looking at me. He thought for a moment, then sighed like a half empty balloon losing air.

"One of two things," he said.

Darina looked up at him concerned.

"Darling, can we not talk about this now," she said patting him on the thigh.

He didn't look at her. He was still gazing through me.

"He tried to kill me," he said, "and you don't want to talk about it?"

It was a rhetorical question and his voice was calm.

"No, I don't want to talk about it," she said.

"Well, now's as good a time as any," he replied.

Genevieve bit her lip and looked into her cup, before looking back up at her father.

"Mother banished him," she said. "That's good enough isn't it, Daddy?"

She was full of hope, like the hot air in a balloon.

"My sweetheart," Lucius said, "your brother, the degenerate, tried to kill me."

"Well, it is a family tradition," said Darina, not thinking before she spoke.

Lucius turned ant looked at her. His eyes burned hot, but he remained calm.

"Don't start with that," he said.

"Well, you did kill your own father," she said, not quite knowing when to stop poking the bear.

"Yes, I did, and I'll kill my own son if I think it necessary," he replied.

His tone was angry now. He got up from the table, walked out of the kitchen French doors, and sat in the gazebo outside. Well played, I thought to myself. Darina scowled at me.

"He can't have it both ways. He is not unblemished, and he is not the sole authority," she said.

I think she was talking to me but I couldn't be certain.

"Yes, I'm talking to you," she said.

Well, there you have it.

Ezra looked over at his mother after taking a good drink from his coffee mug.

"Father does have a point though. Cage did try to kill him."

"Yes, but killing is not going to solve all of our problems. This Killing is small and fragile. Your father seems to have forgotten common sense, which has twice now almost cost him his life. Without Cage, this Killing has only you and him to fend off the evil and diseased vermin. How long can we survive like that, as they breed like virulent leeches?" said Darina.

"I'm not saying that father is correct in thinking of killing Cage, but if he doesn't and he banishes him instead, then is that not worse. Cage could continue to be a problem for us. A dead man makes no travels," he said.

"How can you say that about your own brother?" asked Darina. "Cage is my son and I carried him in my womb for thirteen months. He is not our enemy."

"Well, he hasn't been acting like our friend lately, has he?"

Ezra loved his brother, but he wasn't quite certain of him anymore. Didn't know who he was and what he was now capable of. He didn't quite agree with his father's proscription against interacting with the humans, but he did understand the risks involved.

"Well, he's still your blood and your brother," said Darina, "and as far as I'm concerned, that's good enough."

"Bad blood," said Ezra.

Genevieve didn't like the cross words and the fractured family tree, one limb torn off in this brooding storm.

"We should give him time and space," said Genevieve, "perhaps his banishment will be punishment enough and he'll learn from his mistakes."

She looked and smiled at her older brother. A cherubic, beautiful face. Ezra looked at her but he did not mirror her smile back to her.

"Perhaps," he said.

He got up and went outside to talk to his father. Genevieve and Darina sat in silence for some time.

"The Lafayette boys," said Genevieve, "they're so difficult, Mom, you should have had more girls."

That cleared the air and Darina and Genevieve laughed together.

"I just wish they were as wise and even tempered as you, my darling," said Darina.

Outside the sky had powdered its blue face with cotton swatches of white. It was going to be another glorious day in New Orleans. It was going to be a balmy and clear 82 degrees.

"How do you know that?" asked Ezra.

"It's what the paper said," I answered.

Ezra paid no attention to me and turned to his father. He was seated next to him.

"What are you going to do with Cage?" he asked.

Lucius looked up towards the house where Phoebe was coming out from the kitchen carrying the daily paper. He waited until she had delivered it and he thanked her. She went back into the house, wearing a housemaid's uniform of blue with an apron of white.

"What would you do about him?" asked Lucius.

"I would banish him until he repented. Truly repented. But I'd make the banishment known to the Council of Vampyri so that he cannot receive support from any of us anywhere."

"You are wise beyond your years," Lucius said.

"Well, he's not yet wise, but I hold out hope for my younger brother," answered Ezra. "He is still only a baby."

Lucius nodded.

"Yes, he is. He is not even one hundred years old," he said wistfully.

And although the physical maturation followed a human's for the first twenty one years of life, the wisdom that came with age often took much longer. In fact, a vampire was not considered of age, or an adult, until they had reached their first millennium. As such they held no political powers, voting powers or sway in the government of Vampyri until they turned one thousand years old.

"I do worry about him. His reliability and trustworthiness. You were never like that," said Lucius.

"Speaking as his brother, I do believe he has promise."

"Then we will give him some time to find himself, if that is what he needs."

Lucius picked up the newspaper. He turned to the City section.

"I'm famished," he said. "Let's see what's on the menu."

"Whatever you feel like, I'm happy to quench with you."

One of the main news stories was about Sergeant Christopher Gambino, who had been charged with three counts of sexual assault, causing bodily harm as well as statutory rape of a sixteen year old girl.

Sergeant Gambino was a fifteen year veteran of the New Orleans Police Department. All charges against him were dismissed. They were dismissed because he and some of his cronies had intimidated the witnesses and victims. He was still up to his tricks, and even though he had been assigned desk duty, it was known that he snuck out sometimes on shift and continued to stalk his prey.

On the front page of the City section there was a picture of a smiling, arrogant Sergeant Gambino, just leaving court in his dress uniform. They had a quote from him too:

I'm just happy to have been acquitted. What those women have been through is truly horrible, but to blame it on a career police officer is unconscionable. I'm glad to be able to finally move on with my life, to continue serving the great city of New Orleans, and to carry on protecting her people.

That was the worst piece of scripted crap I had read in quite some time.

"I agree," said Lucius. "I think I've found my supper."

We sat around for the rest of the day watching the sun cut an arc in the blue sky. The shadows grew and then retreated as night drove them off in fear. Lucius got up and walked around the garden at times, but he was not as vigorous as I had seen him. He still had a fair bit of healing to do. The day was leisurely. Ezra went out for the afternoon to enjoy some of the sights and run some chores.

It was after dinner, around eleven p.m., as we all sat around the living room together enjoying each other's company that Lucius spoke.

"I'll be going out for a bite," he said, smoking a pipe, which is something he did occasionally.

Darina looked up from her Sudoku puzzle.

"What do you have in mind?" she asked.

"There's a tasty Italian morsel on the New Orleans Police Department's menu," he said.

"Should you be getting involved with the police?" she asked, worried again.

He looked at her, biting the bit on his pipe. He occasionally smoked his Briar Oom Paul when he was particularly contemplative. Nobody protested; the smell of pipe tobacco was pleasant.

"Well, if they're as bad as the criminals, then I'm going to cull the herd. Whether they walk the thin blue line or not," he said. "So long as anarchy doesn't overrun humanity we can go about our business undetected. But if humans start coming unglued due to violence or crime getting out of hand, well, we might end up having to fight them and the Lobison. That's not something we want."

He puffed on his pipe and a snake of smoke curled up around the side of his face.

"So what did this police officer do?" asked Darina looking back at her Sudoku puzzle, biting on the end of her pencil.

"He's a violent rapist."

Lucius cradled the Oom Paul's bowl in his right hand. It was a warm wooden belly of thoughtful contemplation in his palm.

"I'm going to take Ezra with me," he added.

Ezra looked up at his father and swirled the tea he had in a mug in his hand before taking a sip. It was a cup of chamomile.

"I'd prefer if Ezra stayed home tonight with Genevieve and me," said Darina. "I'd feel safer if he was around. You never know what Cage might be up to, and until the dust settles, I'd prefer that."

"Okay," said Lucius, "it's just me and you then." He was looking at me.

"I wasn't that hungry anyway," said Ezra.

Lucius smoked his pipe for several minutes more, until it was all but finished.

"Well, we'll be getting along, then," he said.

He got up and kissed his wife on the forehead and then did the same with his daughter.

"Goodnight. Don't wait up," he said.

We went into his study and he sat behind the desk. He reached into a drawer and took out a voltaren not much larger or thinner than a piece of paper. It was heavier, though. He laid it on the desk in front of him and pushed a corner of it. It came to life and he tapped some buttons and Vampyri alphabet letters and a holographic screen appeared between us.

He dialed in to this evening's date and then zoomed in to New Orleans. He swiped another screen in front of him and brought up Sergeant Christopher Gambino's image and a ton of information about him. He hacked into the police database and accessed his fingerprints.

It was going to be harder to isolate him, seeing as we didn't have any DNA to identify him by. But the voltaren, this super computer, would be able to get us close, if he was leaving finger prints anywhere.

Lucius input the fingerprints into another program and waited. He swiped the second screen away and got back to the first, which was an aerial view of New Orleans. We waited a moment. Blue dots started popping up all over the map but clustered around the police department and Sergeant Gambino's residence. After a short while the blue dots stopped popping up. The voltaren was now sorting them by most recent.

It was just after midnight. The image in front of us turned thirteen blue dots red. These were the most current fingerprints it had isolated. Each one was dated with the time and day. One of them had 00:01. Lucius tapped on that and it zoomed in. It appeared that this fingerprint was on the outside of a driver's car door. We zoomed in closer. Lucius tapped on the license plate image and sure enough, it was Sergeant Gambino's late model sedan.

"Okay, where are you, Gamby?" Lucius said to the screen.

The funny thing was that his car was parked in Uptown. Far away from the neighborhood of Timberlane where he lived. There was probably only one reason he was here. This was where his first victim lived, in an apartment complex, on the third floor. Lucius zoomed in to her apartment. It was a block from where he had parked.

In infrared view you could see a man walking up towards the complex. There was no one else on the street. Lucius zoomed in even closer. With the night vision option you could tell it was Gambino. He was wearing police hatch gloves. He was definitely up to no good.

"Time for some fine dining," Lucius said.

Lucius took a couple of small sleeping darts out of the drawer. They were the size of a baby fingernail, highly accurate and could bury themselves into human flesh through several layers of clothing. They could kill or put you to sleep within three seconds. They also left no trace of themselves once they entered the body. It's not as painful as it sounds. You hardly felt it at all. Just a small pinch. I figured this was for Nadine Johnson, the woman Gambino was going to visit.

"Spot on," said Lucius.

We left the house and entered the garage and got into Lucius' black S65 AMG. Lucius hadn't taken his dirk dagger.

"I am to quench on him, not kill him," he said.

That was really the same thing, but I understood what he meant. He aimed to kill him by draining not by slicing and dicing. Lucius nodded.

The Mercedes roared to life and we left the mansion. We could have apotrepinated but what with Lucius recuperating we were saving our strength.

"My strength," he said to me.

It only took us about five minutes to get there, driving leisurely so as to not attract attention. We parked a block away, driving up slowly to the curb to reduce any engine noise. We were an opposite block away from where Gambino had parked. No need to make things more complicated.

We walked up to the front of the apartment complex and Lucius looked up at the third floor. He scanned it for a minute using vampire's infrared sight to see inside.

"He's inside," he whispered to me.

He grabbed onto me and we apotrepinated into the one bedroom apartment. We arrived in the living room as Gambino slowly and carefully walked into the bedroom. He was a big man. I put him at about six foot five and around 250 pounds. He was obviously on juice.

We walked into the bedroom behind him and the floorboards under the carpet creaked. He turned around and looked at us, surprise written on his face.

"What the fuck," he said a little too loudly, waking sleeping beauty.

Nadine woke with a start, pulled the blankets up around her and screamed hysterically. Lucius reached into his pocked and, with vampire speed, dispatched a dart at her. It landed on her neck and the next moment she was sleeping and quiet again.

Gambino took a swing at Lucius. He was nowhere near quick enough. Lucius ducked under the punch and came up hitting him square in the solar plexus lifting him off the ground several feet.

"That might have been too hard," said Lucius under his breath.

Gambino dropped to the floor, landing on his back. His eyes were bulging and his mouth was agape. He was trying for air, but his diaphragm wasn't working. He was scared. It was all over his face, like a contorted mask.

Lucius knelt down beside him and placed his hand on his chest, feeling his heart. It was pounding fast and hard. Good, he thought to himself. He wanted him alive for the quenching.

"I'm here to kill you," Lucius said.

He got no reply. Gambino was only concerned with trying to suck in air through thin wires. He was gasping and heaving. Making quite a show of it.

"You know why. You're a bad man, and to make it worse, you cloak yourself in the authority of law. You are the lowest of vermin... well, almost, you're the lowest of the hairless vermin. Any last words?"

Lucius smiled at him. Gambino was slowly drawing his breath.

"I can change," he said, gasping between each word.

"No, you won't," said Lucius. "And besides, it's too late."

Lucius reached under his neck and by his throat and pulled, him up, helping to stand him. He bit into his neck and quenched deeply. Within a few minutes Gambino was dead and his wine sack of skin was empty of blood.

Lucius licked his lips and put the big man over his shoulder.

"Do you have to comment on every little thing?" he said.

"I'm creating ambiance," I said.

Lucius rolled his eyes. He looked over at Nadine, went up to her and put his fingers on her throat. Her pulse was slow but steady.

"Good," he said, "she'll awake in the morning thinking she just had a bad dream."

We apotrepinated right out of her bedroom and back beside the car. Lucius placed him in the trunk and we drove off home. Gambino would be incinerated that night if we were smart about it.

"We are smart about it," said Lucius.

We made it home before one a.m. and the house was quiet. Not even a church mouse could be heard stirring. I helped Lucius carry the body, or should I say, I was with Lucius when he carried the body, into the crematorium out back and fired it up. The process would take around three hours for cremating the remains and then pulverizing the remaining bone fragments and ash. Lucius took off the gold chain that Gambino had been wearing. It would be placed in his study with some of the other mementos he had kept from his quenchings.

Interestingly, if you are the curious type, Gambino, weighing around 250 pounds, would create around 220 cubic inches of cremains for Darina to use in her garden. This is roughly equivalent to filling up a gallon container. The rule of thumb, which is on the generous side, is that one pound of flesh or body weight will convert to one cubic inch of cremains.

I went off to bed and left Lucius with the burning man body. I was bushwhacked.

"You haven't done anything except stand around watching," he said to me.

"True," I said, "but you have no idea how tiring it is trying to paint you in a good light."

I grinned at him and he slapped me on the shoulder.

The next morning was uneventful. Lucius was up before any of us. Bright eyed and bushy tailed, as the humans say. Though he had no tail, his eyes were bright and blue.

I found him outside in the gazebo enjoying the daily paper and a large mug of coffee. He was wearing the same red shirt he had worn last night on his quenching. He smiled when he saw me, taking another sip of coffee from his coffee mug. The mug had an inscription on it: Vampires <3 <3. Vampires heart heart. The last heart was the classic love image of a heart.

"No news on Gambino?" I asked.

He shook his head.

"I don't think they'll realize anything for a couple of days, at least. And they're not going to find anything except his car, someplace is shouldn't be."

Phoebe came out of the house carrying a tray. On it was fresh squeezed orange juice, some brown toast, a pat or two of margarine and scrambled tofu, which looked somewhat like scrambled eggs. She placed it in front of us on the table.

"Thanks, Phoebs," Lucius said.

"There's lots more inside if you'd like me to bring out more?"

Lucius shook his head.

"No thanks, I think this'll be just fine."

He winked at her in thanks and she walked back up the garden path and into the kitchen. Darina came out and joined us. She took a glass of orange juice and a piece of toast which she buttered with margarine. She took a couple of generous scoops of tofu scramble and piled them thickly on the toast. She shook salt and pepper over its face and dug right in.

"You've got a good appetite," Lucius said.

She chewed her food and swallowed. Drank some juice.

"I know, I'm absolutely famished," she said, "I really need a good quenching."

Vampires could not live on bread and water alone. Lucius and Darina both raised their eyebrows at me.

"What," I said, "it's true."

"How was your quenching?" Darina asked through a mouthful of food.

"Good," Lucius said, "but he was definitely on juice, it gave me a bit of a belly ache during the night. Nothing serious, I just noticed. I could also taste it, but other than that, he was healthy. The blood was good."

Ezra came out carrying a small box. He placed it on the side of the table by Lucius.

"This came for you just now," he said.

Lucius looked down at it quizzically. Darina had prepared him some tofu scramble on toast and he was just about to tuck in.

"Interesting," he said, "I wasn't expecting anything."

With his nails he sliced open the tape holding it together. There was no return address on it. He couldn't see inside it, because whatever was inside was the same temperature as the ambient environment. He sniffed at it, but it was full of unknown smells, the most overpowering being the decaying smell of rotten meat, which was the pungent and oftentimes unpleasant smell of humans.

He opened it and inside was crumpled brown paper. He took that out and placed it on the floor next to him. He peered inside. Then he pulled out a thick lock of black hair. He placed it carefully in front of him. Darina looked up puzzled. Then he pulled out a photograph. He placed that in front of him. Darina startled.

"No!" she said, looking at the photograph.

Next, Lucius pulled out a small piece of paper that was lined and looked like it had been torn out of a small notepad. There was a handwritten image on it that was in small, unkempt script. He looked at it for a while, reading it to himself.

"What does it say?" asked Darina, visibly upset.

Lucius looked back down.

"It says, 'we have your son, Cage. If you want to see him alive again you will bring us three million dollars in 4 week Treasury bills. You will wait for our call and deliver the T-Bills to us on Friday."

Today was Tuesday. It was ten a.m. In an hour and a half the auction for 4 week T-Bills would take place. We would be issued them on Thursday. Lucius had to call his bank and make sure they ordered him enough.

"Yes, thank you, I'm very well aware of that," he said.

Darina put her hand to her mouth.

"We have to get them the money," she said.

"That boy has caused us nothing but trouble," said Lucius, with very little anger in his voice. He was surprisingly Zen and calm about the whole thing.

"I've had a close call with death," he said, "that has given me some perspective."

The lock of black hair had to be Cage's. The photograph was of his face. His face was tilted slightly down but his eyes were looking at the camera. His disposition was calm and he didn't seem to have many injuries. At least, not many around his face. There was a chunk of hair missing from the right side above his forehead. This was obviously the chunk of hair that Lucius had pulled out of the box.

Darina reached over to Lucius and put her hand on his wrist.

"You will get our baby back safe and sound, won't you?" she asked.

Her eyes were misty and wet. Lucius looked at her for a while and then he looked back down at the picture of his son with a chunk of that curly Lafayette mane missing. Lucius nodded slowly at the photograph, and pushed his finger into it.

"I will get him back safe and sound," he said, looking back up Darina. "Don't worry."

"I will help you, father," said Ezra.

"Yes, you will," Lucius replied, "for we are about to unleash a horrible end to the people, or Lobison, who have had the gall to do this, thinking they can get away with messing with the Lafayette Killing. They are in for a big surprise."

Lucius walked inside to make a private call to his banker from his study. When you have well over 100 million in investments with a bank, you get special favors. They would courier the T-Bills to him on Thursday afternoon after they had received them. No questions were asked, one of the reasons he banks with them. Oh yeah, the other reason is because they're owned and operated by the Vampyri. I should've said that. The bank, in case you're looking for somewhere very safe to keep your money, is Magnanimis Banking and Brokerage. They might be in the telephone book as MBB.

On Wednesday, Ezra made a special trip to the local blood bank. He brought home forty pints of AB+ blood. The rarest blood of humans was also the most energetic for vampires. They poured the blood into a large silver cauldron made for such a purpose. They tossed in the silver vascin that Doctus Emilio Davidyan had given them. They let the blood mature for three hours and then they feasted on it in the evening.

They drank goblet after goblet of the blood, until their bellies were full and they were energized. Ezra had depleted the blood bank of AB+ blood. There would be questions asked, though the story wouldn't make it into the papers. Robbing blood banks was something the vampires seldom did because it begged questions that humans couldn't answer, and which would gnaw at them like a dog at a bone. But this was a special occasion. The whole family would go on a killing spree on Friday, or as soon as they could, to rescue Cage.

On Thursday the courier came round at three thirty-three p.m. with a large cardboard box for Lucius to sign. Lucius signed for it. He took it inside to the living room table and opened the box in front of everyone. Inside was a large black leather briefcase. It was immaculately polished and soft to the touch.

He opened it up on the living room table to find it filled with T-Bills.

"Looks like it's all here," he said.

He didn't count it, but they were in denominations of one thousand dollars and it looked like there were about three thousand inside the briefcase. Ezra swayed on his feet. He had his left hand cradled in his right palm and he was rubbing his chin with his forefinger and thumb. His eyes were burning hot.

"I want to get those bastards," he spat at the floor.

Lucius came round and put his hand on his shoulder.

"It will be your pleasure, my son," he said.

"I also want to rip their heads off," said Genevieve gesturing with her one hand on top of the other, as if she were literally pulling heads off dolls. It looked kind of strange, coming from the usually quiet and very ladylike, Genevieve.

"I can kick ass, too," she said to me.

"Yes, you can, my darling," said Lucius, "and you will have your chance tomorrow, all going well."

At just after five p.m., Lucius's smartphone rang. The ringtone was the opening, driving beat from Concrete Blonde's song "Bloodletting." He looked at the caller ID, but it wasn't a number he recognized.

"Should I let it go to voicemail?" he asked with a smirk.

"Just answer it, already," said Darina.

He picked it up leisurely.

"Department of the Treasury," he said.

Ezra snickered.

"Do you have the T-Bills?" asked a male voice that wanted to sound strong and authoritarian but was cracking like cheap champagne flutes.

"I have them."

"Good. On the east side of Audubon Park, across from the Northern tip of Bird Island, is a clump of three trees, just by the lake. There is a metal garbage bin there. I will mark it with a blue x. Put the treasuries in there."

"They might blow away," said Lucius, feigning all seriousness.

"Don't fuck around, you know what I mean. Use a suitcase or something. We will be watching. Don't bring any police. Come alone."

"When will I see my son?"

"We will leave him at the Audubon Park Golf Course's clubhouse. But only if you don't try to screw us over."

"When?" asked Lucius.

"At midnight tonight," said the voice.

"The park is closed at that time."

"You'll figure something out."

"Let me speak to my son," said Lucius putting his smartphone onto speaker.

There was a bit of noise and in the background you could hear someone say, "speak to your father."

Then Cage came onto the phone.

"Mother, Father, you have to do as they say or they'll kill me."

"Are you okay, sweetheart," said Darina.

"Yes, but they're serious, they're gonna hurt me if you don't get them the money..."

Cage was cut off and the voice came back on.

"That's all. Be there or your son will die."

The line disconnected.

"Charming," said Lucius. "We have a date, then."

BROKEN HEART

Darina was wearing the floorboards thin with her pacing up and down the living room. Her long dress danced around her ankles as she walked up and down with her thumb in her mouth biting it. She was very worried about her baby boy, Cage. It was written all over her face.

Genevieve had made a nice light meal for dinner of salad with nuts and seeds and a delicious creamy garlic dressing. Darina didn't have the appetite for any food. She was frantic and full of nervous energy.

"You should try and put something in your belly," said Lucius.

She looked at him and smiled nervously.

"I'll be okay," she said, "I just want to get this over and done with."

"It's still another six hours or so until we have to get to Audubon Park," he reminded her.

She nodded and went back to biting her thumb and fingers as she turned around and paced back towards the fireplace.

Lucius nodded to me and we went into his study. Ezra followed us in. Lucius closed the door.

"Okay," he said, "this is how we're going to get these naive werewolves or whoever it is that thinks they can mess with the Lafayette Killing."

He opened up the briefcase that held the T-Bills and placed it on one side of his desk. He took his voltaren out of the drawer and placed it on the desk in front of him. He pushed a corner of it and it came to life. He tapped on some of the keys written in Vampyri and a holographic screen appeared vertically from the voltaren.

"I'm going to take these T-Bills and pass them through here," he said pointing to the holographic wall emanating from the voltaren, "and scan them. Each T-Bill, made from paper and ink has a unique signature, as you know."

Ezra nodded. I nodded too, though I didn't know that they had a unique signature but it made sense. Lucius waited.

"When you're finished," he said, "I'll continue."

I rolled my hand out in front of me. Continue your royal highness.

"No need to get snarky," he said, "but these are serious times. We are here to rescue Cage, and his life might depend on it."

"Sorry," I said, "I'm all ears."

"So what will happen," continued Lucius, "is that our computer will pick up the unique signature from each of these T-Bills so that we can identify them using the satellites in orbit and the signature of each one. If they split the T-Bills up between them we'll still be able to track each and every one."

Ezra nodded. He was pensive, looking slightly down, resting his chin on his thumb and forefinger.

"We're not doing this so that we can get the T-Bills back, though hopefully that will be a nice side benefit. No, we're doing this, so that these bastards cannot hide anywhere. If they split up, so long as they have a T-Bill with them, we'll find them," said Lucius.

Lucius smiled and licked his lips. He was looking forward to vengeance again. It had been a while since I'd seen him this energetic. It was good to see.

"Why not just find out where Cage is right now, with this DNA?" asked Ezra.

"Well, son," said Lucius, "I want this whole package wrapped up nice and easy. If we go after Cage now, who's to say we find all of the culprits responsible for this mess. I'd prefer to let them take the T-Bills. That way, they'll think we are playing by their rules. It will give them a sense of control they don't really have and it will feed their greed. Once they have the T-Bills, they'll get greedy. You know how werewolves are, they can't help but salivate over the thought of easy riches. Much like people. So, I am pretty certain that once we have given them the money, they'll all come together to celebrate, maybe get drunk, and then we strike with all fury."

Ezra nodded steadily.

"I like it," he said.

I did too.

"Go get yourself prepared, son," said Lucius. "I'm going to take some time to scan through all these three thousand T-Bills."

"My pleasure," said Ezra as he left the study.

I stayed with Lucius as he telekinetically took each T-Bill and passed it through the holographic scanning wall of the voltaren. Each time he did, it came through the other side and floated down to rest across from the computer. Each T-Bill's unique signature was captured as it was scanned and shown in the upper corner of the holographic screen. It flashed a blue border as it finished before blinking off and the next one started scanning through.

Each T-Bill only took two to three seconds to be scanned.

"Who do you think might have kidnapped Cage?" I asked him as we sat in his study, and I found myself bored watching the T-Bills being repetitively scanned again and again. He looked at me before replying.

"That's hard to say for certain. I'd guess it is the Lobison," he said.

"But you practically decimated the Galvez pack not that long ago. In fact, Bernardo took off with his tail between his legs."

Lucius nodded.

"True," he said, "but I've learned never to underestimate these vermin. They are quick to call upon their friends and allies. I wouldn't be surprised if this is Bernardo seeking revenge."

"Yeah," I said, "I suppose it makes sense that it would be them."

"Well, who else do you think it could be?" he asked.

I looked down at my feet and wiggled my toes. The top of my shoe moved up and down slowly.

"I don't know, some crazed lunatic who thinks this is an easy way to get some money from one of the wealthiest families in New Orleans," I offered.

"Then they are, as you say, crazy. No one in their good mind would mess with vampires," he said.

"Agreed, but nobody knows you're vampires," I said. "So they have no idea who they are messing with."

Lucius thought for a moment. I think he thought that I had a good point. And I did, I thought I'd carry on while I was ahead.

"New Orleans is still recovering from the great Hurricane Katrina," I said. "There are a lot of desperate people who are hard up and need some money. And they'll try and get it any way they can."

"I think you're bored," he said. "You might be right, but they'll soon see the error of their ways. I like your cafe philosophical take on these things. But really, what good is it going to do to offer up opinions when we'll soon find out."

I shrugged.

"Well, we could make it fun," I said. "How about a Benjamin as a wager on this."

He smiled at me like a confident grandfather.

"Careful now," he said, "I'm not that old. A Benjamin it is. But just so we're clear. You think it is some crazy citizen or group of citizens and I think it is the werewolf."

I nodded.

"Yes, and by citizens, it could also be one of the crime gangs around here," I said.

"Okay," he said offering me his hand. "You have a deal."

We shook hands. We both grinned at each other thinking the bet was already won. I left after watching the mind numbingly boring scanning of T-Bills go on for over an hour. At that point, Lucius was about half way through them.

I went to the dining room and sat down to the meal of salad that Genevieve had so nicely prepared. Phoebe came in to see if I wanted anything to drink. I took a sparkling water. Genevieve was sitting down with me.

"I can't wait for this family to get back to normal," she said.

I smiled carefully. I had forgotten what normal was.

"You know," she said, "having everyone back again, living under one roof. Enjoying happy times together."

She picked at some salad greens on her plate. I wasn't sure how a family that goes about killing can ever expect to have a 'normal' life together.

"That's because you don't quite understand us," she said to me without animosity in her voice. I smiled at her again.

"I think tonight we'll have your brother back safe and sound," I offered.

She nodded.

"Of that I have no doubt, but Daddy is going to be so upset. I don't think he's forgiven Cage yet and so he's probably going to banish him at the very least," she said.

I put a forkful of salad in my mouth. The taste was marvelous, creamy and garlicky. One of the best salads I had enjoyed ever. I told her so. She beamed and thanked me.

"Well," I said, "you can't expect him to get over something like his own son trying to kill him very quickly. Can you?"

She shook her head.

"I suppose not, but Cage is my brother and he's just very confused at the moment. I don't think he really meant to kill Daddy."

Sometimes I wasn't sure if Genevieve was really naive or if she just wanted to believe in fairy tales. We finished the rest of our dinner in silence. When we were almost done, Darina and Ezra came in to eat. At least Darina was going to try and eat something.

Under his right armpit, Ezra had holstered his Glock. Under his left armpit were three additional magazines. With one in the gun already, I figured he was carrying 45 pieces of lead. He was strictly business.

"Tonight will be a bloodbath," Ezra said, "nobody messes with my brother and gets away with it."

Darina put some salad on her plate and asked for a glass of orange juice when Phoebe came back around. Ezra requested a sparkling water like me.

Darina had changed and was wearing a pair of sensible slacks and flat shoes with a good grippy sole. Similar to how Genevieve was dressed. Only Genevieve was in black slacks and Darina had on gray slacks. They both had on white blouses and black jackets. Underneath their jackets and holstered under their left arms they both carried Charter Arms Pink Lady .38 Specials. In each pocket of their jackets they carried a loaded 5-shot speedloader.

I had none of their toys and felt quite naked next to them.

"How is the scanning going?" asked Ezra.

"He should be finished in the next ten to fifteen minutes I think," I said looking at my watch.

I helped myself to another heaping pile of salad greens. I was feeling quite hungry. The excitement always gave me an appetite.

"That's because you just sit around and watch, like you're watching a movie," Ezra said.

"Maybe I should bring popcorn then," I said.

Genevieve giggled. Darina sighed.

"This waiting is killing me," Darina said. "I just want to get this over and done with. The family has given me too much anxiety these past few weeks. I'm going gray before my time."

She pulled at one of her hairs on her head and brought it in front of her face to look at. It was black as coal. She didn't have a single gray hair on her head.

"Nice of you to say," she said to me. "Still, this is all too much excitement. It's making me dizzy."

"You love it, Mom," said Genevieve.

Darina smiled at her.

"I might, if it wasn't your brother we were trying to save. He's been a very naughty boy, lately," she said.

Lucius came in. He had dressed for success too. He was in all black. Black slacks, black shirt and black overcoat. Underneath his overcoat, strapped to his thigh, and around his waist on his right side was his Dirk dagger with a red bloodwood handle. From his back pockets protruded two red leather driving gloves. He always wears a splash of red.

"All set Father?" asked Ezra.

Lucius nodded and sat down. He heaped a big pile of greens on his plate. He looked around at everyone.

"I see you're ready, too," he said.

They all nodded.

"My ladies look absolutely ravishing for a night on the town," he said to Genevieve and Darina.

"Thank you, Daddy," said Genevieve.

"Stop it," said Darina playfully, "this is serious."

"Yes, it is," he said.

He dug in to his meal. Phoebe came by and took my plate and asked Lucius what he wanted to drink. He asked for sparkling water.

"So, on a more serious note," said Lucius, "this is how I want tonight to go down. We'll all head up to Audubon Park in the Mercedes. I'll park us at the end of Prytania Street, by the entrance to Audubon Park. I'll take the briefcase with the T-Bills up to the garbage by Bird Island. I'll leave it there and come back to the car. We'll wait at Prytania until we receive a call that Cage is safe near the Audubon Park Golf Clubhouse. We'll go pick him up, and once we have him, then, and only then, will we start looking for our vermin. Any questions?"

"Don't you want to wait by Bird Island to see who picks up the briefcase?" asked Ezra.

Lucius shook his head.

"No, we don't need to do that. The scanned T-Bills will get us to our culprits."

"What if they take the money, Daddy, and don't leave Cage by the clubhouse?" asked Genevieve biting her lip.

Lucius looked at his only daughter and smiled.

"I don't think that's going to happen," he said, "and if it does, we'll find Cage because we'll have the T-Bills to show us the way."

"But what if something happens to Cage before we can get to him?" she asked again.

"Don't worry my darling. Nothing is going to happen to Cage. He can take care of himself, and these bad guys aren't going to risk doing anything to Cage, at least until they have their money. And when they see that their money is all there, they're not going to have any reason to hurt your brother," said Lucius.

"And we won't let them, Gen," said Ezra, "we'll kick their asses, right?"

Genevieve smiled and nodded her head.

"Try not to worry yourself, my love," said Darina patting her daughter's hand. "I trust your father, and he won't let anything happen to Cage."

She smiled up at Lucius, partly in hope, partly in belief.

"I've given this a lot of thought," said Lucius, "and this is the best way to handle it. Trust me. If we try and nab the werewolf who grabs our briefcase with the money before he gets to his friends, we could lose Cage and then we'll have to spend lost time finding out where he is with the voltaren. In the meantime, he could be in danger if the werewolf pack loses contact with their member who was scheduled to pick up the package. Really and truly, the best way is to wait and bide our time. Let them think they have the upper hand. Let them get their T-Bills and start celebrating. That's when their guard will be down and that is when we will attack. I know we all want to get Cage back as quickly and as safely as we can. But getting him back all in one piece needs to be done carefully."

Lucius looked around at everyone at the table and then he looked back at Genevieve.

"Okay," he said.

"Okay Daddy," she said, "I trust you."

They smiled at each other. I was getting itchy feet just sitting there. I sat and waited while everyone ate their salads, or as was the case with Darina, play with her food, until we got up and went into the living room to watch the grandfather clock get stuck at around nine thirty. At least that's what it seemed like. Time dragged by so slowly I thought I was growing younger by the minute.

At quarter to twelve that evening, Lucius got up.

"Let's go," he said, putting on his red gloves.

He went into the study and brought out the briefcase.

"Is it all there Daddy?" asked Genevieve nervously.

He opened it up for everyone to take a look. Four neat, thick stacks of T-Bills were present and accounted for. We left the house and got into the black S65 AMG. Lucius was driving and took Prytania Street all the way from the Garden District to the end of the line. At this time of night it wasn't more than a five to seven minute drive.

We crept up slowly to the yellow poles at the end of Prytania Street where the road ended and it became a walkway into Audubon Park. He pulled up facing the park with his lights off, on the right side of the road a couple of meters before a fire hydrant and in front of a tan colored Toyota minivan. There were no lights on in the gray house next to us. Nor any lights on in the stony, sand colored house across from us.

"Okay, wait here. I'll be back in less than five minutes," said Lucius.

Darina passed him the black leather briefcase and he exited the car. He closed the door very softly and carefully. We watched him walk into the park and then disappear right after a short time. It was as quiet as death in the car. You couldn't hear anyone even breathing. After a while, Genevieve cleared her throat. We watched like sentinels, staring straight ahead into the blackness of the park. The trees looked dead and gray. Nobody was out and about at this time of night in the park.

About four or five minutes later, Lucius came back.

"Did you find it okay?" asked Darina in a whisper.

He nodded.

"They had painted a blue X on it as they said they would."

Lucius turned the ignition on to accessories. The dashboard clock turned to midnight exactly. Nothing happened in front of us. At seven minutes after midnight a lone figure passed by us in the park about fifty feet from us. He, or she, was wearing a hoody. You couldn't see much else about them.

"He's a male," said Ezra. "I can tell from my infrared vision."

I nodded. TMI I thought to myself.

"Hey, just saying," Ezra said.

"He's right," said Darina.

"That's enough," said Lucius. "Nobody wants to hear about any human's or werewolf's privates."

About five minutes later the same figure came by in front of us running south along the park pathway, carrying the black suitcase. Lucius smiled.

"Good," he said, "everything is going according to plan with those vermin."

"How do you know they're werewolves, Daddy?" asked Genevieve. "I can't smell them."

"Me, neither," he said, "I just have my suspicions, and it's likely that he's downwind from us and that's why we can't smell his stench."

"How long are you going to give them to call, Father?" asked Ezra.

Lucius looked at the clock on the dashboard.

"Well, assuming he's making his way back to the clubhouse, which is probably unlikely as they'll have security checking in every so often, but using that as worst case, I'll give them fifteen minutes."

Lucius twiddled with the front central COMAND controller which had been tweaked to contain a Vampyri voltaren. The screen lit up and a holographic image was projected a few inches away from it, and enlarged. It was roughly twelve inches diagonal.

"Let's see where our Huckleberry is going," said Lucius.

He tapped on the holographic image and a satellite map showed up. It gave our location as a blue dot and not far from us was a little red dot moving down Perrier Street. That was the street south of us. Lucius zoomed in and we watched from a bird's eye view about a hundred feet from the ground as our Huckleberry climbed into a white panel van parked on Calhoun Street by Coliseum. They drove off slowly and carefully, heading down Calhoun. We watched them stop by Magazine Street before turning right onto it.

"I think they're heading to the clubhouse," said Darina.

They slowed down as they came up to the exit into the Audubon Park Golf Clubhouse but they didn't turn into it.

"Curious," said Lucius.

They kept on going down Magazine Street.

"Maybe we should start following them," said Darina.

Lucius shook his head.

"No, we'll give them a bit of time. Maybe they don't have Cage with them and they need to pick him up."

"I knew we should have put his DNA into the voltaren," said Darina, "then we'd know for certain where he is."

"That's not how we behave," said Lucius. "Our privacy as vampires is one of our most sacred rights. We can't ignore that right until we know for certain that Cage is in danger."

Darina looked out the window. She knew he was right, but she was still upset.

"We have to obey the Vampyri sacred rights, Mother, you know that," said Ezra.

Darina nodded.

"I know," she said.

"We'll get them," said Lucius, squeezing her gently on the thigh. "Just a little bit of patience. We'll make no mistakes on this one. I promise."

We waited for fifteen minutes, watching the van drive towards Bucktown. Off of Poplar Street the van turned left onto Aztec Avenue. It pulled up onto a driveway about halfway down the avenue on the left hand side as we looked at it from a bird's eye view. The picture was clear but it was dark and everything was tinted in gray and shadows.

Lucius turned the image to infrared and we saw three people get out of the van. One of them was carrying the briefcase. Inside the house there were an additional five people we could count. The three from the van joined the five in the house. They huddled together in what was probably the living room. All around in a circle. The one who brought in the briefcase opened it up for everyone to see.

They moved around a bit. It looked like some of them were jumping up and they appeared to be giving each other high fives.

"I think we should probably expect a phone call any time now," said Lucius.

We were still parked. We hadn't moved. It was warm in the car. It was warm outside and I was stuck in between Genevieve on my left and Ezra on my right in the backseat.

We continued to look at the voltaren holographic image. A couple of the bodies moved away from where they were huddling and entered what appeared to be the kitchen. This Vampyri technology was quite high def infrared, considering what you've come to appreciate from most infrared examples.

They pulled out a box. Probably a case of beer and took it back to the rest of the group. Beer was handed around and they sat around and probably talked a bunch about how clever they had been and how they'd now be rich. Thing is, they had 3 million dollars between eight of them it seemed. That's not a helluva lot of money.

"That's not your concern," said Ezra.

"Still, they weren't all that smart. Maybe they didn't know how rich you guys are. They probably would have asked for more," I said.

"I wonder why they haven't called yet?" said Darina. "I don't think this is a good sign."

It was now twelve thirty three on the dashboard's clock.

"We'll give them until twelve forty," said Lucius.

Nothing much happened in the house for a while from our vantage point. We watched the clock turn over a few minutes. And just as it went twelve thirty seven, Lucius' phone buzzed. I was glad he had turned off the ringer.

He looked at it.

"I have a text message," he said.

He unlocked the screen and tapped on the message icon. He looked at the message and furrowed his brow.

"Well, what does it say?" asked Darina trying to peer over his shoulder but not having much luck.

Lucius shook his head wearily.

"It says," and he swallowed and coughed.

"Go on," said Darina her voice sounding a little tighter than it did the first time.

"It says," and he coughed again, "'your son is dead. You have been p-w-n-e-d' whatever that means."

"What?" said Darina.

She took his phone from him as he showed it to her.

"No, this can't be true," she said, starting to get very visibly upset.

"What does this mean, this 'p-w-n-e-d?'" Lucius asked.

"It means you've been owned. It is a misspelling of owned and it's pronounced like that with a p at the beginning," said Genevieve.

"Kids nowadays," said Lucius.

"What are you talking about?" asked Darina. "When our son has just been murdered and you're asking about a stupid word."

She started to cry. Lucius took her into his arms.

"He's not dead," he said, "unless they killed him before we got here, he's not dead, we've been watching them this whole time. They wouldn't have killed him earlier. That would just be stupid."

Darina looked at him, trying to dry her eyes.

"You think so?" she asked.

"Yes," he said nodding, "though we should hurry, because that might be what they're planning."

He started the car's engine and it came to life with a deep throaty growl. He turned the car around and sped out of there. His face was determined and his jaw was clenched.

"Excellent," said Ezra, "let's get this show on the road. Time to find out where Cage is and bring a quick end to these vermin's' short and miserable lives."

Eight people in the house and five of us. Though I usually don't get involved, so really it's one against two. Those should be very easy odds for vampires versus werewolves. That's if I was wrong and they were Lobison and not humans. If it was humans, well then, it was going to be too easy for the Lafayette Killing.

It was a five kilometer drive and Lucius was driving it like he owned the roadway. In many ways he did. It was quiet as we zipped onto Bonnabel Boulevard from Metairie Road. The light at the number 10 was red. Lucius slowed down as a courtesy before flooring it through the intersection. The nice thing about the S65 AMG is that it is fast. Fast as a sneeze. Veteran's Boulevard was green for us. A small win. West Esplanade was red, but we had places to go and Lucius zipped in between two pokey vehicles heading west. East was clear.

I was watching the clock on the dashboard. It only took a little over seven minutes. I was pleased with the time. The holographic video of the house showed very little activity. Six people looked to be hanging out in the living room on chairs and sofas. There were two people in a bedroom, and they looked to be making out on the bed from what I could tell.

"Aren't they going to be in for a surprise," said Ezra.

Genevieve giggled.

Turning left onto Aztec from Poplar, Lucius turned off the lights and went with his infrared vision. Not that it was that dark out. There were still street lights after all. This was a nice middle class suburb. The lawns were well manicured and the houses well kept. They were pretty little boxes, but with not so pretty little faces inside.

Lucius pulled the car up to the side of the curb on the right hand side and turned it off. We were parked halfway on the grass. Thankfully the grass wasn't wet, or Ezra might have complained about getting his boots wet. He looked at me with a frown.

"Okay," said Lucius, "we're going in fast and hard. You see that house down there on the left, the third house down, red in color?"

We all nodded. The van was parked on the driveway, barely off the street.

"That's the house. We'll walk down together until we get to the last house before it. Then I'll give you a three second countdown like this."

He put up his three fingers and then slowly folded each one back down into his fist in turn.

"When I drop that third finger we all apotrepinate inside the living room. Attack whoever is closest to you. Show no mercy. I will ask the questions of anybody closest to me and find out where Cage is. If I'm not done, whoever is done first, deal with the two in the bedroom. Understood?"

We all nodded. I had butterflies in my stomach.

"Me, too," said Genevieve.

"Okay, let's go," said Lucius. "Don't draw your weapons until we get inside the house. I don't want any nosy neighbors being concerned. Though, it looks like everyone in this sleepy suburb is asleep. Good for us."

"Let's make this quick, Father," said Ezra, "the noise of gunfire will wake up the neighbors and we don't need the cops on our tail."

Lucius nodded. We all got out of the car and closed the doors softly. We crossed the street, following Lucius as he looked both ways. All around us the houses were under cover of dark night and smoky street lamps. I could see no lights on in any of the houses as far down on both sides of the street as I could see.

We crept along the sidewalk trying to look as if we were neighbors just out for a midnight stroll and some fresh air. We walked softly and made hardly any sound. The rubber soles of our boots absorbed the sound of each footfall. We passed a brown roofed house and then we passed two gray roofed houses. The next one was where our Huckleberry was.

Lucius stopped and looked into the red colored house. There were still six people in the living room, drinking beer and probably getting wasted. The two lovers were still in the bedroom. He turned around to us and nodded. We were huddled by a large bush, just outside the flooding street lamp.

Lucius put up his hand with three fingers pointed skyward. He dropped his ring finger. He dropped his middle finger and then he dropped his index finger. We apotrepinated into the living room. I felt more butterflies in my stomach. Apotrepination is always such a rush for me.

It was dark inside the room. There was only a little bit of light leaking in from the kitchen. The rest of the living room was bathed in the dull blue from the TV. The sound was pretty loud. It was some sort of talk show. We appeared in gray wisps of smoke off to the side, just where the kitchen exited into the living room. Nobody saw us for a second. Then one of the four males in the room looked over as he was taking a sip from his beer. He dropped his bottle.

"What the fuck!" he said. He brushed his long curly hair out of his eyes.

Everybody else looked over at us as Darina and Genevieve pulled out their Pink Ladys. There were two sofas in an L shape. Two women were on the love seat and two guys were on the three seater. Two other recliners were off to the side of the love seat where another two men sat.

Nobody got up off their chairs for a couple of seconds. Then the two guys in the recliners, two big men got up as if they were pulled up together by puppet strings. They were average height but stocky and bald. Both had goatees. They took a step towards us.

Darina and Genevieve moved forward, fast, like only vampires can, and snuck up behind them. Just as they realized these two ladies were behind them they turned around and that's when they got lead.

Each of them received two .38s from each of
the Pink Ladys. Darina and Genevieve shot them
twice, quickly, just under the left shoulder blade.
Right through the lungs into the heart. The sound
was deafening and startled the other four into reality.
The whole incident looked like a dance movement as
they men turned slowly towards the women, before
slowly dropping down in front of them, sideways.

Ezra seeing that everything was under control
in the living room made his way down the hall to the
bedroom where the two lovers were.

The other two men started to try and get up
off the couch. They both had long hair. The one guy's
was curly, the guy who dropped his beer which now
lay on the carpet spilling its contents. The other guy
had straight brown hair just below his shoulders.
They were struggling to get up off the couch. The
curly haired guy was trying to say something, but his
mouth was just opening and closing as if he was
trying to breathe.

Genevieve and Darina moved almost like one.
They came up in front of the two men, between the
couch and the coffee table. They kicked the coffee
table away and it tumbled into the television. They
helped the two men get up off the couch by taking
their arms and twirling them up. It looked like ballet.
The two men were lifted up out of the couch, wincing
in pain as they stood on their toes. Their arms were
trapped up high behind them and they had their
backs to the Lafayette ladies.

They strained to get free; twisting their necks around to see what was going on. This all happened very quickly, you understand. Up came the Pink Ladys, and in concert, four gunshots almost sounded like two. Darina and Genevieve shot their partners twice each. Just under the left shoulders again and into the heart. Two red buttons. They let the men go and they dropped down in front of them as if in supplication or worship.

"You're exaggerating," said Darina to me as she stepped over the dead bodies and leaned against the wall with Genevieve, as Lucius was already with the two women who were in the love seat.

Lucius had casually strolled up to the two young women who were sitting there while Darina and Genevieve had killed the four men. By this time they were cowering, both with their hands over their eyes. He took his Dirk dagger from his holster and plunged it through one woman's breast into her heart in one swift movement.

His eyes were cold as frozen steel and he was determined. The other woman, with scraggly black hair started to whimper and cry. He picked her up under her right arm with his left, holding her high at a funny angle. She looked like a limp doll. Her free, left arm hung by her side. She was in pajama bottoms and a button down pajama top. It had little red hearts on it.

"Where is Cage?" asked Lucius. His voice was cold menacing and quiet.

She looked up towards Darina and Genevieve. "He's... he's..," she said.

"Where?" asked Lucius again, his tone colder and louder this time.

She blinked tears from her eyes and sniveled.

"He's... he's in the bedroom," she said, looking down again.

As Lucius let her go, he brought up his dagger again and slashed it deeply against her throat. Her legs at first caught her fall before they gave out as her throat gushed a stream of blood from her artery. It streamed past Lucius like a red ribbon, and as she fell she twisted and turned and her blood spurted out again like a fountain and then once more like an incompetent dribble. She hit the floor and the angle of her head opened up her neck and the rest of the blood seeped out like a large puddle as the carpet did its best to sponge it up.

Lucius turned around to head down the hallway to find his son as he put his dagger back in its sheath. As he started down he saw his two sons heading toward him. Ezra was pulling Cage along by the elbow and Cage was coming involuntarily. A woman came out from the bedroom behind the two of them.

"I saw him screwing that wench in the bedroom, with the suitcase of T-Bills on the bedside table," Ezra said.

Lucius looked at him, confused for a minute.

"These are my friends, Father, what have you done?" yelled Cage, looking past Lucius and at the carnage in the living room. Darina and Genevieve were in the hallway now, crowding in behind Lucius.

"What are you saying, son?" asked Lucius.

Cage didn't know when to shut up. That had often been his problem. He looked at me scowling.

"This was my idea, okay. I wanted to get the hell away from you and your stupid vampire ways," said Cage.

Lucius blinked his eyes and furrowed his brow. Still not quite sure what had happened, but slowly the magnitude of this event was unfolding in his mind.

"Me and Jenna are getting the fuck out of here, and leaving for good. Look at what you've done. You've killed my friends because of your stupid ideas of purity and your asinine rigid rules."

Cage jerked his elbow out of Ezra's hand and reached behind him for Jenna's hand. She had a bed sheet around her.

"You mean to tell me that you orchestrated this whole kidnapping so you could get your hand on a measly three million dollars?" asked Lucius, half incredulously.

Cage nodded.

"Don't act all surprised. You never gave me anything and you've asked for so much in return. I'm tired of living under your rules and dictatorship for these 97 years. I'm leaving and I'm taking my girlfriend with me and you can't stop us."

Cage made an effort to move past his father but Lucius stopped him.

"And, I'm gonna tell the cops what you did here tonight," Cage added.

"No, you won't, son," said Lucius forcefully.

"You damn well better believe I will," Cage answered back.

Cage pushed his way through past his father. Jenna clung to his hand for dear life. As she came up next to Lucius he thrust his hand up into her just under the solar plexus and pulled out her heart. Cage felt her drop behind him as she tugged at his hand. He turned around to see what had happened.

"Here, take her with you," said Lucius and he tossed Cage her warm, wet heart.

Cage involuntarily caught it and looked down at it. It took him a split second to recognize what he now held in his hand.

"Noooo!" he yelled at his father.

He flew at him and they crashed against the wall at the end of the hall. Lucius was still not as strong as he should have been. Cage launched them up through the ceiling and they crashed down on top of the beams in the ceiling. Lucius picked up his son and smashed him down through the ceiling and beams, landing them on the floor. Cage was quick to get up and he grabbed his father and tore him through the wall and into the kitchen cupboards.

Cage grabbed a knife and slashed at Lucius, nicking him across the cheek. He slashed at him again as Lucius put up his hand and the knife cut across Lucius glove, cutting him in his left palm. Lucius grabbed Cage's wrist and bicep and broke his elbow over his knee. Cage screamed in pain.

With his good hand, Cage tore at his father's face, leaving three deep slashes across his forehead and over his cheek. He picked up his father and smashed him back down breaking him through the kitchen sink. Water started squirting out through both the hot and cold pipes.

Cage took this moment to apotrepinate out of the house. He reappeared a block away on Live Oak Street.

"We've got to get him," said Lucius, getting up tenderly and carefully.

The rest of his family was looking at him.

"Come on, let's go," he said again, holding his left shoulder which had been dislocated in the fight. He attempted to walk towards the front door.

"I'm not going with you," said Darina.

"Me neither, Father," said Ezra.

He looked at them quizzically and opened his mouth to admonish them again when the sound of police sirens could be heard coming closer.

"Damn," said Ezra, "we took too long and we made too much noise."

"Okay," said Lucius, "we apotrepinate a couple of blocks away and then we'll have to apotrepinate back into the car."

He was holding his right upper arm with his left hand. He stretched out his three fingers again, wincing a bit. He wrapped each of the fingers around his bicep again in turn. The three of them apotrepinated out of the house.

"The T-Bills," he said to me. We went back into the room. The T-Bills were all in the suitcase we grabbed it and closed it.

"Ready?" he asked.

I nodded and closed my eyes and when I opened them we were standing on the corner of Sigur Avenue and Poplar Street.

We watched the first of five cop cars skid around the corner onto Aztec Avenue. Its lights and sirens off by this time. Right behind it was another cop car. Then a few minutes later two more. A fifth cop car came up from Live Oak Street.

"We need to move quickly," said Lucius. "Apotrepinate carefully, we need to reappear really quickly, really quietly, into the car."

"I'll drive," said Ezra.

Lucius nodded.

"Now," he said.

The next moment I was sitting in the backseat of the Mercedes on the left hand side. Lucius was on the right hand side. Ezra was in the driver's seat and Darina was in the passenger seat. Genevieve wasn't there. Then she arrived, reappearing between Lucius and me.

"Thanks, Daddy, you could have given me a countdown," she said.

He put his finger to his lips. I was a bit nervous, sitting out here in the open somewhat. We had no choice, I knew that. We couldn't just leave the car on the side of the road for the cops to grab; we had to take it out of there. In hindsight we should have parked a couple of blocks away like we usually do. In our defense though, we thought this was going to be a slam dunk. Turned out a little differently.

"How about a little bit of optimism from the peanut gallery," said Ezra in a low whisper.

About a hundred and thirty feet north, down Aztec Avenue, the last of the cops was getting out of his car, and with pistol drawn, he was approaching the house we had just had our spree in. He disappeared out of our line of site in front of the neighbor's bush.

"Now," said Lucius.

Ezra started up the engine and it came to life quietly, but louder than we would have liked. He kept the lights off and backed out into the intersection slowly. We had parked on the east side of Aztec so we now needed to head west along Poplar in order to get home. Not ideal.

Instead, Ezra reversed onto Poplar and kept it in reverse as he went east along Poplar for about fifty feet. There were no other cars on the road. Thank God for small mercies. Then Ezra did a U-turn in the middle of Poplar and headed east again, but this time in drive and in the proper lane. Smart man.

"Thank you," he said.

"That was unnecessary," said Darina.

Ezra looked over at her.

"Who are you talking to, Mother?" he asked.

"Your father."

"What?" asked Lucius, he was still holding onto his right arm. The briefcase on his lap.

"That was unnecessary, Lucius," she said again and a little more loudly.

"What was?" he asked.

"Pulling her heart out of her chest like that in front of your son," said Darina. "Even though she might only be human, your son still had feelings for her."

"She's only part of the sheeple," he said to her, "and Cage needed to be taught a lesson. He's been running around with those damn humans for too long. And we couldn't just let her live now, could we?"

"All I'm saying," said Darina, "is that you should have been more discreet. Now, you've upset Cage and he isn't likely to come back anytime soon."

"Good," said Lucius. "It's that, or I kill him the next time I see him

WARMONGERS

The 1940s were a tough time for the Vampyri. I suppose you could say they were a tough time for humanity too, but this is a story about vampires and especially the Lafayette Killing, and as such, I'm more concerned about the Vampyri than I am about humans. Though having said that, what affects the Vampyri in a detrimental way, also affects humanity in a detrimental way.

But, before we get to the 1940s, or the swinging forties, I need to get you up to speed about the Lafayette Killing. Our vampire heroes.

"That's a bit pompous, don't you think?" said Lucius to me.

"Not really, you are the hero of our story. At least that's how I'm trying to describe you if you'll let me do my job," I replied.

Lucius raised his eyebrows at me and went back to reading the Times Picayune. On the front page was the maddening as well as saddening story of a mother killing her two children. These were babies, practically. The son was four and was shot in the head and then drowned in the bathtub. The daughter was five, and because the gun misfired, the mother drowned her in the same bathtub which still held her brother. I was hoping Lucius would go quenching on that bitch.

"Maybe," he said to me, looking up from his paper. "If it'll make you feel better."

"It will," I said.

And there I was getting derailed by the day's news. It's no wonder that I prefer not to read or watch news. Nothing but bad news. No good news whatsoever. No stories about young men helping little old ladies across the road or things of that nature.

"Doesn't sell," said Lucius.

"They don't know that," I replied. "They've never even tried."

"I don't know why you're so upset," he said. "We head out every week, going somewhere to look for trouble and we always find it. If there were no werewolves and no criminals, what would we do with our time? More than that, how would we justify the culling we do of the human herd? We'd have to be killing and quenching on good, decent, common folk. That's not a world I really want to live in."

He had a point. With all the pain and misery that humanity was inflicting upon itself, it helped vampires keep a low profile. Add the brutality of the Lobison, or werewolves, with the idea of vampires being "real", and it all just seems ridiculous to humanity. As it should, as the Vampyri Killings prefer it to be.

So we sit here in the living room. Lucius reading the depressing paper and me just mulling things over in my mind. Everyone in the Lafayette Killing was dispersed across the house doing their own thing.

I could hear Genevieve off in her crafts room sewing her next masterpiece and in the same large area, Darina was painting again, a picture of Vampyr, her home, from memories she still kept alive. If it was up to her, they would have returned home by now. But it wasn't up to her. It wasn't really up to Lucius either.

I mean, they could request a transfer back, but Lucius liked it here, and he had been here most of his life, anyway. In many ways Earth was home to him. He was a big deal on Earth, the vrykolakas, or head of perhaps one of the most prestigious Vampyri Killings in this arm of the galaxy. A god amongst men in many respects.

"Let's not get ahead of ourselves," he said.

And Ezra was off in his room, watching some sort of reality show. It gave him no end of entertainment watching the humans bicker and squabble and fight amongst themselves in their curious and intimately human small mindedness.

And that leaves Cage, Lucius' youngest son. Lucius looked up at me and furrowed his brow. I was expecting him to say something but he didn't. He went back to the paper, turning the page. I think it still smarted him, having his son try and blackmail him in concert with those human friends of Cage's.

It was, perhaps, the ultimate betrayal. A betrayal that Ezra as the firstborn son would likely never even imagine contemplating. But Cage had been difficult for years. You think they'll grow out of their infantile stages, and you never imagine they'll turn on you like Cage had done.

Lucius had promised to kill him if he saw him again. I'd hate to see that. Though it would be understandable and well within Vampyri law. But I was fond of Cage and I really thought there was potential for him to make something of himself. To become a really productive and influential member of not only the Lafayette Killing, but perhaps even the Council of Vampyri.

But that was not my jurisdiction, nor something I would have any say in or sway over.

"Not true," said Lucius, turning to look at me, "you know I value your input and wisdom greatly."

Perhaps, but Lucius seemed to have made his mind up quite quickly.

"I make my mind up all the time," he said. "Doesn't mean I don't change it from time to time, or say things in the heat of the moment that I later reconsider."

I nodded at him. Dracula, their French Bulldog, was sitting at Lucius' feet. He had his eyebrows raised and his chin on his paws, which were crossed in front of him. He seemed to be listening and mulling the conversation over in his head. If only he could talk. I wonder what he would say. Perhaps Dracula would suggest giving Cage a chance.

"Perhaps," said Lucius, as he reached down and scratched Dracula behind the ears.

But Cage had been given many chances. He had already twice tried to kill his father and now he had tried to blackmail him by ransoming his own life. If Cage wanted to repent he was showing no sign of it. And a sincere repentance would have to come before any thought of reconciliation could be entertained.

"Or maybe," said Lucius, "Dracula would bite Cage's arm off, wouldn't you boy, yes, you would, yes, you would."

Lucius was talking to the dog in doggy speak. Dracula, in spite of his name and his bat like ears, was not a monster or a vampire. He was as harmless as the tooth fairy. But absolutely adorable and loving.

Darina came downstairs in her nightgown.

"I'm heading up to bed sweetie," she said to Lucius. "Are you coming to bed soon?"

Lucius shook his head.

"No, he's got a bee in his bonnet about a mother killing her children this morning, so we'll be heading out for a quenching."

He was meaning me. But there were no bees in the house. Darina came up and kissed Lucius on the mouth.

"Come on, my baby," Darina said to Dracula, patting her thigh.

Dracula got up without hesitation and followed Darina upstairs to bed. Lucius put down the newspaper and turned on the television. The eleven o'clock news came on. We waited for the story about the infanticide, which was one of the top stories.

"A New Orleans woman from Gert Town was taken into custody this morning for allegedly killing her two children. Ms. Bronty Shawnison is expected to appear before a judge tomorrow to address these charges," said the TV news anchor.

"There you have it," said Lucius.

The video accompanying the voiceover was of the main court and police buildings downtown. She'd likely be in police custody overnight. It wasn't a Friday or Saturday night, thankfully, which means that the holding cells would likely be emptier. And I was pretty certain that with a murdering woman like her, she would likely be given her own cell, if they had the space. And they probably had the space.

"We'll wait until early morning. Perhaps around three a.m.," said Lucius.

"Sounds good to me," I replied.

So we sat around watching late night television and biding our time. Genevieve came by at around eleven thirty to say goodnight and to kiss her father before she went off to bed. Shortly after that I nodded off. I was woken by Lucius gently shaking my shoulder. The house was dark and quiet. The time on the grandfather clock had just gone three a.m.

"It's time to head out," he said.

I got up and we got ready to go. Lucius was dressed in black pants and a black long sleeve shirt. He had on a red belt and black shoes with red shoelaces. Around his wrist he had on a voltaren. We walked out to the car together and drove off to Gert Town. It wasn't a long drive. No more than five or so minutes. Lucius drove us up to the apartment building where Bronty Shawnison had, until this morning, lived with her two children and parked at one end of the complex.

It was dark and quiet outside except for the smoldering streetlights. Lucius looked around. He was being cavalier about pulling up right in front. He surveyed the apartment complex trying to figure out which apartment had belonged to Bronty.

"Okay, you ready to go?" he asked me.

I nodded. He grabbed me on the wrist and right from inside the Mercedes S65 we apotrepinated into a dark apartment. It had been carefully ransacked. I say carefully because that's how the police ransack a place after a crime.

Lucius walked into the bathroom and found a comb, which is what he had come looking for. He took a piece of hair from it and came back out into the living room. Sitting down at the kitchen table in a rickety chair, he turned on his voltaren and dropped the hair over top of it.

He brought up a holographic screen from the voltaren that stretched out in front of us to about thirteen inches. He tapped away at the holographic screen and a map of New Orleans came up. A blue dot appeared in the main police building downtown. He zoomed in and, inside a cell adjoining other cells, the image of Bronty came into view. She was lying down in an orange jumpsuit on the bed in her cell. Apparently sound asleep.

Lucius moved the image around, both horizontally and vertically. The police station was rather busy. He counted half a dozen police officers dotted around the jail area.

"We're going to have to apotrepinate in and then quickly out again bringing her with us. This is going to take some finesse," he said.

I could see what he meant. I was starting to think that this whole vengeance thing of mine was not such a good idea.

"Vengeance is mine, sayeth the vampire," said Lucius.

"And what about the abduction?" I asked. "We can't really explain that away can we?"

He shook his head.

"They'll just have to deal with it," Lucius said, they meaning the humans.

However, it was still going to create a problem. You can't enter like a ghost into a jail and make someone disappear, only to have them wind up dead someplace else, without questions being asked.

"Doesn't matter," said Lucius. "They can ask all the questions they want in the world and they'll never find the answer. Vampires are beyond humanity's feeble brain to comprehend and understand."

Still it made me a little nervous. Maybe I shouldn't have opened my big mouth.

"And besides," continued Lucius, "I'll bet you a hundred bucks that they'll cover this up. There is no way this is going to make it into the papers. A woman disappears out of police custody and ends up back in her apartment dead. How do you explain that? You can't. So what'll probably happen is that they'll bring her back into the cell and say she committed suicide there."

So now I knew where Lucius was going to quench. It was a poetic touch, bring her back to her own apartment, where she killed her own children, to meet her own death. I liked it. And Lucius made sense. There was a slim chance of this killing making it onto the news.

"Ok, let's go," he said.

Without waiting for my affirmation, Lucius grabbed my arm and we apotrepinated back into the car. I felt a little giddy.

The drive to the police station and cells wasn't far. We pulled into a parking lot along the street right beside the jail. Lucius turned on his voltaren again to confirm where we were in relation to her cell. We were a little off. Lucius drove up a couple dozen more feet. We were right below the holding cells and out of the view of a street light.

I was getting nervous. The thing I liked about the Mercedes was that it was black in color and the windows were tinted black, too. You couldn't really see inside the car unless you came up and pressed your nose against the windows. Even then you needed good eyesight.

"Wait here," he said.

I wasn't upset to be waiting in the car. I nodded my agreement. The next moment, Lucius had apotrepinated out of the car and I was left with nothing but a swirl of charcoal gray smoke that dissipated almost as quickly as it arrived.

Lucius reappeared right inside her cell. It was dark, the only light that came in leaked in from the hallway. He ducked under the camera that was in the one corner of the cell by the door.

He opened up a holographic screen in front of him and tapped into it. Then he took a small cartridge, one that looked like a tiny watch battery, from his voltaren and attached it to the camera above his head. This would tap into the main computer feed that was recording this camera and sending it to the monitoring room, and it would loop the last hour of video of Bronty as she lay in her cell. This little piece of voltaren technology would then self-destruct after ninety minutes in a puff of smoke. I loved Vampyri technology.

Lucius looked back at the holographic screen emanating from the voltaren on his wrist. He tapped at the screen and an image of what the police officer monitoring the video from this cell was shown. It showed a sleeping Bronty. Lucius waved his hand up in front of the camera. Nothing appeared on the image he was viewing.

Lucius nodded to himself. It was all set. He went up to Bronty and put his mouth down by her pulsing neck. He bit into it and just as she came to she was put under again by the vampire's anesthetic and paralytic agents. Depending upon the anesthetic a vampire chooses to use, the victim will either remain conscious or unconscious.

Lucius picked her up and apotrepinated out of the cell arriving right by the trunk of the car. He opened it up and put her in. Nobody was around to see. Then he climbed into the front seat and looked at me.

"That was easier than I thought it would be," he said. "She's sound asleep, like Sleeping Beauty."

"She's no Sleeping Beauty," I said.

He grinned.

"Why so serious?" he asked. "It's just a manner of speech."

He started the car and we drove leisurely back to Gert Town. We parked almost in the exact same space we had left not an hour before.

"Come with me," he said, "I'll try and apotrepinate the three of us from just behind the trunk. Might be tricky."

We got out of the car and made our way back to the trunk. Lucius looked around. It was just after four a.m. Nobody was around. All the lights in the neighborhood as far as we could see were out. Lucius opened the trunk and took a hold of Bronty's hand. He grabbed my hand. The next moment I found myself in dissipating smoke feeling giddy. We were back in Bronty Shawnison's living room. Lucius laid her down on the soiled and threadbare couch.

We each pulled up a kitchen chair and watched her.

"What are you waiting you for?" I asked Lucius.

"Better days," he said, grinning.

"Seriously?" I asked.

"Well, you're the one who wanted this. Don't you want to try and get some sense of closure? Some sort of understanding as to why she killed her kids? If not, I'll just get on with it. Just thought I'd offer you the chance," he said.

I nodded.

"Yeah, I suppose I wouldn't mind trying to understand the sickness that made her kill her children."

So we waited just a few more minutes as Bronty started to come to. She stirred and her head moved slightly. Then her eyes fluttered open and she looked at us for a long few seconds. Trying to figure out where the hell she was. Then she tried to get up, but the paralytic agent was still strong in her veins.

"Who the fuck are you?" she asked.

Lucius shook his head slowly, from side to side.

"Tut, tut," he said, "that's not language for a lady to use."

Bronty's eyes got bigger as fear started to creep up her spine like a spider looking for a soft place to lay its eggs.

"Who the fuck are you?" she asked again.

I guess some people just couldn't help themselves. It was the way they were brought up or the way they learned to speak. I didn't care. Lucius and I had heard worse language than this before.

"He's the Lone Ranger," I said, "and I'm Tonto."

Bronty squinted and furrowed her brow at me.

"The lone what?" she asked.

She didn't get it, and I was getting tired. It was after four in the morning and my own cuteness was wearing thin on me.

"We're lawman," said Lucius, putting on his best, deep cowboy impersonation, which he actually does quite well.

I snickered. Bronty started to get up on her elbow. She put her palm against her temple.

"If you're lawman then I should be in jail and this ain't no jail. This is my home," she said.

She was starting to sound a little more confident. I couldn't tell if that was the effect of the anesthetic wearing off or she was just getting cocky.

"No, this isn't your cell. This is your last five minutes of life," I said. "Why did you kill your children?"

She started to cry then.

"My poor babies, my babies, I'm sorry," she said.

She was rocking herself back and forth, and then quite quickly she darted towards us, trying to make a quick escape between the two of us. The problem is, she didn't realize how fast vampires were.

In an instant, Lucius was on his feet and his hand was held out in front of him at an angle. Bronty was dangling from the end of his hand by the throat. He opened his mouth and his vampire incisors unsheathed. They were long and sharp like needles. He hissed at her.

"Jesus," she said, and her eyes were bulging white hard boiled eggs with rotten brown yolks in their center.

"Lone Ranger," he replied back to her, but she didn't get it.

A stream of urine snaked down her inner thigh and puddled on the carpet beneath her. Lucius was maddened and repulsed by the frailty and vileness of humanity.

"Tonto, here, asked you a question," he said to her. "Answer it."

She dangled from his arm like he was holding nothing more than a frayed piece of yarn. Her feet swayed ever so slightly in their blue jail issued slippers.

"My babies," she said. "I didn't means to kill them."

She started babbling incoherently. It was hard to understand her.

"I don't think we're getting anywhere," Lucius said to me.

I nodded. My eyes were heavy. I didn't care about the answers anymore. I cared more about my own sleep.

"I agree, kemosabe," I said.

And with that, Lucius brought her throat up to his mouth and bit deeply into it. He quenched for a second and then pulled his mouth from her throat. He spat out several ounces of her blood onto the carpet.

"Vile," he said. "Absolutely vile. This disgusting human is sick and diseased. Her blood is nothing but a cocktail of drugs and mental illness."

He spat at the floor again. He tossed her over his shoulder as the anesthetic and paralytic had once again taken hold. He walked into the bathroom and put her in the bathtub.

"This is where you will die," he said, looking at her. "Where you killed your children."

She looked at him with big eyes. She was still conscious. They were riddled with fear. He turned her head towards him to expose her left carotid. He slashed it open with his nails and then pushed her deeper into the tub and tilted her head away from him. The blood spurted out against the white porcelain bathtub. We watched for several seconds until the heart stopped pumping. Her orange jumpsuit was now a mottled red and orange.

I looked down at her and I had feelings of misgivings. For her, death was painless due to the anesthetic administered by Lucius' vampire incisors, but I perhaps, would have preferred her to suffer, like her children had suffered.

"Revenge is not always the sweet, tasty morsel of success," offered Lucius. "Sometimes it's about culling future violence."

I nodded. This was not a tasty morsel. But I was glad to see it meted out. Lucius took me by the arm and we apotrepinated back into the car. We drove home, leisurely, each of us immersed in our own thoughts. I had a feeling Lucius was a little miffed about not getting a good quenching.

"No, I'm not," he said. "There are plenty of sheeple in the pasture."

I dragged myself into bed as soon as we got home and I slept like a tired, blissful baby.

The morning came too soon. The light seeped in through the windows like acid burning the backs of my retina. It was just after nine a.m. when I finally got myself out of bed and headed into the kitchen for the sweet salve known as coffee.

Lucius was already there reading the paper. He looked up at me.

"See," he said, "not a squeak about Bronty going missing. I told you they'd keep it on the down low."

I nodded and poured myself the largest mug of coffee I could find. I sat down and looked at the tablecloth. I drank some of my coffee. Lucius had recovered marvelously from his fight with his son. His shoulder was back in its socket and his slashes and bruises were all healed.

"I'm feeling like a million bucks," he said

"More like three million in T-Bills," I answered back.

He chuckled.

"Yes, three million T-Bills. Speaking of which, I'm going to take them back to the bank to be deposited in my account," he said.

He folded the paper and placed it on the table.

"I think I'll get going soon. Do you want to come along?" he asked.

I had nothing on the agenda for the day so I nodded my head.

"Sounds like fun," I said.

"I'll go and get the briefcase," he said.

He left and headed into the study. I drank my coffee and then I had another one. Darina came downstairs and said good morning.

"How was your snack last night?" she asked.

I grinned. I didn't snack.

"She was vile," I said. "I think Lucius was upset about it."

"I was not," he said, returning into the kitchen.

Darina and Lucius kissed each other on the lips. He asked her how she slept. She said she slept well.

"Speaking of money," I said.

"We weren't speaking of money," Lucius said to me.

"Well, earlier we were, and I'm a bit slow this morning. Anyway," I said, "you owe me a Benjamin I believe."

Lucius looked at me quizzically. Darina raised her eyebrows.

"Not again," she said to him.

"What?" he asked.

"Don't get into bets with him, you know you'll lose nine times out of ten," she said.

She winked at me. I chuckled proudly.

"Pride comes before a fall," said Lucius. "And what do I owe you the money for."

"Cage's blackmail," I said. "I told you it would be sheeple not Lobison."

Lucius nodded.

"Damn you," he said in jest, "that's right, you did say it wouldn't be the vermin."

"I wonder how he's doing?" Darina said softly.

"Who?" asked Lucius.

"Cage," she said.

"I'm sure he's fine," said Lucius.

"Well, he has no friends. We killed them and he's all alone and hurting," she said.

I was about ready to excuse myself. I didn't like where this was going.

"Please Darina," said Lucius, "he's not an infant anymore. He's twice now tried to kill me and he's tried to rob us too. He's getting exactly what he deserves."

"But he's my baby," she said.

"Your baby, who tried to kill your husband. What about some sympathy for me," said Lucius.

She put her hand on his forearm as they sat next to each other at the kitchen table.

"My sweetie, Cage really doesn't have a chance of killing you. Not while you're in your prime like this. You make it sound so much worse than it is. Really, he's just a boy and you're a man."

It was true. Cage wasn't really a viable match for Lucius, at least not when he was in tip top shape like he was now.

"I thought you were trying to portray me as the hero here," he said to me. "This is not going to help."

"Sure it will," I said. "They want to see the sensitive, vulnerable side."

He rolled his eyes and turned back to Darina.

"I'm sure he's fine. If you want, we can put word out to the Council of Vampyri for the other Killings to keep a look out for him. But if he's found, then he needs to be exiled to Orleans. At least for a while," he said.

Darina nodded and kissed him on the cheek.

"Maybe," she said, "if we don't hear from him for a few days."

"We?" asked Lucius. "I doubt I'll hear from him at all."

Darina didn't say anything to that. It was true, and sometimes the truth didn't need repeating. Lucius reached into his pocket and pulled out a wad of bills. He took one off the top and gave it to me. A nice clean Benjamin. I smiled at the old man's face on the bill.

"Good doing business with you," I said.

"Not at all," replied Lucius, "the pleasure is all mine. You ready to go?"

I nodded.

"Give me a few minutes to shower and change."

I left Darina and Lucius at the kitchen table. Ezra came downstairs to join them. He kissed his mother on the cheek.

"Anybody heard anything from Cage?" he asked after sitting himself down with a cup of coffee.

"Your mother and I were just talking about that," said Lucius. "We haven't heard and your mother is quite worried."

Ezra took a sip of his coffee and looked over at his mom.

"I'm sure he'll be in touch. I don't think he has anyone else now after our visit," said Ezra.

Darina nodded.

"I hope so," she said.

"Perhaps you can find out if there is any word on the street," said Lucius.

Ezra nodded and drank some more coffee.

"I will," he said, "though I don't have much connection in the nether world."

"Well," said Lucius, "go ruffle some feathers then and see what starts squawking."

Ezra smiled at his father.

"So you want me to find out where he is so you can go and kill him?" asked Ezra.

Lucius looked at him coolly.

"Let me worry about your brother's punishment," he said. "He tried to kill me."

Ezra shook his head.

"No, that's not how I remember it father. He left after he had smashed you through the kitchen sink. You were still very much alive. And besides, Cage isn't strong enough yet to be a match for you."

"What, is this a conspiracy where I'm allowed no sympathy from my family?" asked Lucius, half-jokingly, half-seriously.

"No, father, but really, you had to pull his girlfriend's heart out in front of him? Then toss it to him like it was an apple?" asked Ezra.

Lucius shrugged.

"Maybe it was a bit melodramatic, but he's been warned before. Why can't he be a good lad like you? Why does he continue to cavort with the sheeple?" asked Lucius.

"You don't know that I'm not cavorting with sheeple," said Ezra, smiling.

"I do," replied Lucius. "I've had you followed."

Lucius smiled wickedly. Ezra's smile dropped off his mouth silently. Lucius grinned even more widely.

"I'm kidding, son. I'm just kidding," said Lucius laughing.

"That's not funny," said Ezra as he stuck the smile back on his face.

I came back into the kitchen. Lucius stood up.

"We're taking the T-Bills back to the bank. Anyone want anything while we're out?" he asked.

Ezra and Darina shook their heads.

"Drive safe," said Darina.

We left and got into the car. Lucius was in blue jeans with a white t-shirt with a big red heart on it. The heart was bleeding. Oh the irony.

"Listen," he said to me, "you've got to keep a sense of humor or you'll die of boredom as an old grump."

We drove down to Magnanimis Banking and Brokerage. MBB is a very secure banking institution. They have over 33 trillion dollars under management. You're not supposed to know that. But they're trusted by governments around the world, sheeple as well as the Vampyri. The Vampyri making up the lion's share of that contribution.

It could be a lot more. But then it would just get hard to hide, and besides which, the Vampyri have limited need of money and that's only when dealing with sheeple.

"Some things are better not shared," said Lucius.

So I'll keep quiet, then. Anyway, MBB is extremely secure. Vampyri get special treatment and the bank manager showed Lucius into his private office. Lucius handed over the suitcase.

"It's still all here," Lucius said.

"Back into your regular account?" asked the manager.

"No. Put it aside in a discretionary account just in case," said Lucius.

"Very good," said the bank manager.

"One other thing," said Lucius.

"Anything," said the bank manager.

"Put word out about my son. I'd like to find him," said Lucius.

Lucius pulled out a picture of Cage from his back pocket and showed it to the bank manager.

"I'll send the details along later," said Lucius.

And with that we left the bank. The bank manager as you'd probably have guessed is Vampyri. Not as highly ranked as a Councilor at the Council of Vampyri, he nevertheless had connections within the Vampyri international banking community and therefore the vampire community at large. Bank managers were extremely helpful in an assorted concierge sort of way.

"Why don't you start telling them about the forties," said Lucius as we drove home.

I nodded. The forties, as I mentioned before, were a tough time for the Vampyri, and for the world in general. Specifically, I should say that the period from 1939 to 1945 was a difficult time. You'll know this period of time as the Second World War of humanity. It resulted in the death of over 50 million sheeple, and likely many more, depending on who's doing the counting.

That's a lot of culling. Mostly it was the herd culling itself, but it was instigated by the Lobison. And this is where the problem for the Vampyri came to be.

To understand the Second World War, you really have to understand the First World War and how that started. You see, the Lobison, or werewolves, have been involved since both they and Vampyri arrived around 12,000 years ago. But this is not a history text, nor is it about the First World War. Perhaps we'll talk about that at a later date.

In any event, the beginnings of the Second World War can be understood, for our purposes, through the Treaty of Versailles which was imposed upon Germany by the Lobison. These Lobison went by the names of Lloyd George of England, Vittorio Orlando of Italy, Georges Clemenceau of France and Woodrow Wilson of the USA. You will know these men as the statesmen and leaders of their respective countries at the time.

The only non-werewolf amongst the lot was Friedrich Wilhelm who you might know as Wilhelm II, the German Emperor during the First World War. So it is no surprise that the Lobison chose to make an example of him and try him for war crimes.

Now, I'm not saying he was a saint. In fact he was probably rightly tried for atrocities against humanity. However, you have to understand that as a human, he was the chosen scapegoat of the Lobison during the Treaty of Versailles.

And here's the problem as far as the Vampyri are concerned. The werewolves of George, Orlando, Clemenceau and Wilson were a gaggle of smaller packs that just happened to gain power and weren't of much concern to the vampires. But this Treaty of Versailles, which they set up, created an opportunity for the powerful Goebel pack to take power and terrorize the world, leading to many problems for Vampyri and many Vampyri deaths to boot.

You'll probably know one of the Goebel pack just by name, Joseph Goebbels. But the leader is Adolf Hitler and he's the alpha of the Goebel pack that we aim to decimate.

In a nutshell, the Lobison under Adolf Hitler are aiming through the Second World War to decimate the Vampyri and if they aren't stopped, the Vampyri's domination of Earth could be in serious jeopardy. So Lucius is going back to Rastenburg, East Prussia—which is now mostly Poland—on July 20, 1940.

If you've been a student of humanity's history you'll know that on July 20, 1940, some stupid sheeple tried to blow up Hitler and some of his commanders in a botched attempt. Lucius will be heading back to finish the job, or at least complete the job before the sheeple have a chance to botch it.

Some of you might think that this whole idea that Hitler was a werewolf, indeed, the alpha of one of the most vicious and powerful Lobison packs in the history of Earth, is nothing more than a fairytale. And that's how we'd rather you view it.

But know this, Hitler's own chosen nickname of "wolf" was not chosen by chance. And this Wolfsschanze or "Wolf's Lair" where his bunker is hidden is also not named by chance. And for the very curious, his first name, Adolf, is from Old High German meaning "noble wolf". Not that there is anything noble about the vermin known as Lobison. I give you this additional information for further thought.

What I share in these pages is not mythology or fairytales, even though believing they are might give you comfort on dark, cold nights. No my gentle humans, there are dark wars being fought all around you, and your only hope of continued life is through the benevolence and power of the Vampyri being able to keep, in a very real sense, the wolves from the doors.

"I think that'll do nicely," said Lucius.

We arrived home to find the family out in the garden.

"How was the bank?" asked Darina.

"Not a hitch," said Lucius, "I put in a word for the manager to pass along information about Cage. They'll be looking for him."

Darina smiled.

"Thank you, my love," she said.

Lucius bent down and kissed her on the forehead.

"We're going to get ready for an errand," Lucius said.

"What sort of errand?" asked Darina.

Darina was seated in the gazebo with Ezra and Genevieve. They were enjoying some tea and cookies.

"I'm going to assassinate the Goebel alpha leader," said Lucius.

He spoke as casually as someone might about boiling an egg. Ezra raised his eyebrow at his father.

"You mean you're going to try and kill Hitler. Have you gone mad, Father?" he asked.

"No, I'm bored, and it's about time someone took care of the Goebel pack," replied Lucius.

"But darling," said Darina, "we have tried to take care of the Goebel pack before, unsuccessfully. You know that. Don't do this without passing it by the Council."

"I don't need their permission," said Lucius coolly.

Darina was worried, as was Genevieve. I didn't blame them. I might have mentioned that the Goebel pack was one of the most powerful Lobison families that had stained this Earth. And yes, the Vampyri had sent a Killing in to try and annihilate the Goebels and they had failed.

"Whose side are you on anyway?" asked Lucius.

"I'm just saying we need to be careful," I said.

"And who said you're coming along," Lucius said to me.

Truth be told, I could find my own way there. In any event, what I was going to say before I was so rudely interrupted was that the Vampyri had not sent Lucius Lafayette to kill Hitler. And if any vampire was capable of decimating the Goebel pack it was Lucius.

"That's more like it," Lucius said.

I smiled at him thinly. As weak as Darina's tea.

"Well then, if your mind is made up, I'm coming with," said Ezra.

"No, you're not," said Lucius.

"Lucius, don't be daft, you need someone to help and Ezra is your best bet," said Darina.

"I'm taking him along," he said, pointing to me.

Darina looked at me with what I thought was disdain.

"He's useless and not trustworthy," she said.

"You're being unkind," said Lucius. "Besides, my mind is made up and this is just how it is going to be. Besides, it's going to be hard enough getting the two of us into Wolfsschanze. There is no way in hell we'll be able to get three of us in."

"I can't believe this," said Darina getting visibly upset. "You're walking right into the lion's den."

Lucius shook his head.

"No, not at all. We're going to stroll right into the Wolf's Lair," he said smiling mischievously.

Darina shook her head and pursed her lips.

"I don't know why I bother," she said.

"Because you love me," he said to her.

She let escape a small smile, briefly, before putting on her severe face again.

"Be careful, at least," she said, and looking at me. "It'll be on your head if he doesn't come back just like he leaves here."

I nodded at her.

"You're making a big mistake," said Ezra.

"We'll discuss it when I get back," said Lucius.

"If you get back," said Ezra under his breath.

"Oh, ye of little faith," said Lucius.

Genevieve got up and came around from the far side of the table in the gazebo. She kissed her father on the cheek.

"Please be careful, Daddy," she said.

"I will, sweetheart," said Lucius. "I'll be back before you know it."

And with that we walked back into the house and into his large study. One of the reasons why vampires don't need a lot of money is because of technology. In the closet in the study was Lucius' vrenolc. A vrenolc is what you'd probably call a replicator, if you're familiar with science fiction at all.

Lucius pushed his thumb on the one corner of the vrenolc and it read his DNA before coming to life. He then brought up a holographic screen, which he tapped into. He chose some mid-ranking officer clothes of the Third Reich. We were both Lieutenant Colonels. Lucius had chosen to be an Army Senior Chaplain and I was given the accouterments of a Senior Field Surgeon. Not that I knew anything about surgery, but Lucius figured we had a better chance of slipping through the cracks as men of the cloth and apron.

I felt German, if there is a feeling to that. At least I felt as I imagined an important German Lieutenant Colonel would feel in the 1940's Germany. Important, stuffy and self-righteous. Funny how putting on clothing can put you in a certain mood.

"Sieg Heil," said Lucius, offering the Hitler salute and tapping his jackboots together.

He was a rascal sometimes, our Lucius. Though his German was perfect and nuanced.

"Yes," I said, "to our victory."

Lucius dialed us in for a TimeDent exit into Wolfsschanze at 12:12 on July 20, 1944. In the pockets of our M43 tunics we had pictures of most of the senior officers that we should expect at the Wolf's Lair on that particular day. Though we were mostly concerned with one Claus von Stauffenberg, it was important that we understood who all the other players were so we could play our part. We also had a map of the Wolf's Lair to help us figure out where the hell to go.

We stepped into the TimeDent and exited into 1944 on a warm July day at shortly after noon. We were behind a clump of bushes and trees. Hidden away from the main buildings.

From our vantage point you could see the buildings quite easily, though they had been well camouflaged from any aerial viewing. The area was naturally thick with bushes and trees which were in full bloom. It was green and fragrant. I looked around us and at the map of the Wolf's Lair. We were just behind the building that held Hitler's adjutants and personnel.

We strolled casually westward towards the conference shack, which was about three to four hundred meters from us. We spoke to one another in German trying to sound buoyant and optimistic about how well the war was going.

Though by this stage, Germany was on its last legs. We smoked cigarettes and greeted fellow officers as we walked by.

It was a brilliant plan to TimeDent right into the Wolf's Lair, because once we were in, there was no real concern. Anyone already inside was apparently vouched for. Especially when you were dressed just like you'd be expected to dress. Not everyone knew everyone else in here, either. There were, by my guess, over one hundred personnel here at any time, and many senior officers would come and go as requested.

We made it into the conference building without incident at just around twelve twenty. We made our way into the conference room, which was already filling up with most of the members who would be in attendance on this fateful day. It would be a full and compact room. This would work in our favor so as not to draw too much attention to ourselves.

We stood in the far left corner behind Adolf Hitler, or at least where he would be when he came in to sit down. In front of us was Franz von Sonnleithner representing the Ministry of Foreign Affairs and General Walter Warlimont who was the Deputy Chief of Staff of the OKW which, in English, was the Supreme Command of the Armed Forces. Neither of these two men would have any reason to know us, or suspect us. Just how we liked it.

At twenty-seven minutes after twelve Hitler came in, followed by several other men, the last of whom closed the main door. Lucius looked around and did a quick head count. Everyone was here, including Stauffenberg, who was standing just behind Lieutenant General Adolf Heusinger who was immediately to Hitler's right.

At twelve thirty on the nose Hitler started the meeting.

"Gentleman," said Hitler, "I have called you all here to determine the best course of action in order to win this war. It is not going well. The allies are making gains in Italy and North Africa. Field Marshal Rommel has been badly wounded. This cannot carry on."

Hitler slaps the desk and a couple of the men next to him startle slightly. Stauffenberg takes this opportunity to leave. Lucius notices that he doesn't have his suitcase with him. Which means it is probably in the lavatory. The Fuhrer is getting upset. And when he gets upset, someone is going to pay. Tonight, four men will lose their lives, one of them being Stauffenberg. Lucius is not concerned about Stauffenberg or the piddly little qualms of men.

What he wants though, is to make sure that Stauffenberg makes it back and that his bomb goes off. The plan is; we'll wait until Stauffenberg gets back into the conference room and places the briefcase under the table. When Stauffenberg leaves we'll make sure he's able to get away if we can help. Lucius and I will leave right behind Stauffenberg and wait quietly behind the conference shack on the south side. Most of the explosion detonates northward.

When the explosion has gone off, we'll apotrepinate into the conference room and in the confusion, Lucius will kill Hitler. It's that simple and that elegant. The rest of his werewolves will not know what hit them for at least several seconds after the explosion. It's perfect. At least we think so.

As Stauffenberg exits, Lucius nods to me and we make our way out, too. We head into the main office area and pretend to be searching for some documents in the briefcase Lucius brought with him.

We watch Stauffenberg head into the washroom. We discuss the blueprints that the Fuhrer needs as a junior officer heads by us and exits the conference building for a smoke break.

Just a couple of minutes go by and General Gunther Korten comes out of the conference room. He looks at us and approaches.

"Where is Stauffenberg?" he asks politely, as only the Germans can.

"He's in the can," says Lucius pointing to the lavatory.

Well, he doesn't actually use the word can, but that's the loose translation of his German. Korten nods and heads into the washroom. We hear him banging on the toilet stall, calling loudly for Stauffenberg.

Stauffenberg acknowledges him and says he'll be right out. About thirty seconds later Stauffenberg exits with Korten behind him. Stauffenberg is looking around nervously. The briefcase is in his hand. If anyone had been paying attention they'd be asking where that briefcase came from. But that's the problem with sheeple, they don't pay attention.

Lucius gives me a soft elbow.

"We don't want things to go wrong," he says.

We get back to shuffling papers. Lucius looks at his watch, really a voltaren, on his wrist. It looks like a 1940's watch. At least today it does. In about two or three minutes, the phone should ring with the fake phone call for Stauffenberg. We head into the washroom to kill some time. Nobody else is around except for two enlisted men in the office, one of whom is manning the switchboard.

We hear the phone ring, and decide to exit the washroom. The young man answers it. Acknowledges the caller and then gets his companion to head into the conference room to fetch Stauffenberg. A moment later, Stauffenberg exits. He's nervous as hell. It's written all over his face. He's sweating too. And yes, it's warm, but not that hot.

He picks up the phone.

"Yes," he says.

"What...You mean right away...But I'm with the Fuhrer...Okay, I understand."

Well played young Claus, I think to myself. Stauffenberg mutters something inaudible and briefly gives us a nervous look. He walks out of the conference building and we follow not five seconds later.

Stauffenberg doesn't look back, walking briskly to his car where his aide, Werner von Haeften is ready. We walk around to the back of the conference building. In about five to seven minutes the bomb should go off. Lucius takes this time to light a cigarette. He doesn't smoke, except for the occasional pipe, but somehow he thought it was appropriate in this situation to start the habit.

"I'm not starting any habit," he says to me. "Vampires aren't affected by tobacco or any of the human's vices."

I see quick movement just behind us. I look around and see Cage coming quickly at us, staring at his father. He takes Lucius by surprise, launching them both up through several tree branches. The branches break and came crashing down.

Cage takes his father and throws him at a clump of trees twenty-five feet away. Lucius crashes against the trunk about fifteen feet high. The tree snaps and topples, falling away from the conference room.

Cage then comes flying at his father, but this time Lucius is prepared. He grabs him and slaps him hard on his back onto the hard ground. I look around, and I can't believe that there are no spectators yet.

"I've come to save you, Father," says Cage, through winded breath.

Lucius has his hand high above his head, ready to slash down and severe his son's head from his body.

"When will you learn?" asks Lucius.

"Honest, father," says Cage, "I've come to save you. The werewolves know you're here."

I look around and a hundred feet away, I see werewolves by the dozens running for us through the forest.

"Open a TimeDent!" Lucius yells to me.

I fiddle nervously with the ring on my finger. I wasn't used to this. I didn't normally do this kind of thing. The werewolves are fifteen feet away when our TimeDent opens up and we fall into it. The last thing I heard as we entered the TimeDent was the explosion of Stauffenberg's bomb going off.

Then I found myself in the Lafayette backyard. Darina, Ezra and Genevieve were still there. I didn't know how long we had been gone.

Lucius was still on top of Cage, his hand ready to slash down at his throat.

"Oh, my God," said Darina in surprise.

"Don't, Daddy, please don't," begged Genevieve.

ABOUT SYLYNT STORME

Ever since I was a little kid I used to fly around my backyard pretending I was a Jedi Warrior or Federation Captain. When I say fly I mean run around pretending I was in a space ship.

Me and my friends used to take wooden rulers and paint and draw elaborate controls on them and these were our joysticks. We had X-wing fighters and USS star ships and we would spend hours exploring alien worlds and getting into dog fights. The good guys always won.

When I got a bit older I started to absorb everything I could about vampires, going through my own goth and vampire stage. I loved how cool they were and how they were sort of like super beings or demi-gods.

Not even werewolves could outfox vampires. These mysterious blood suckers were lurking around every dark corner of night, just waiting to pounce on unsuspecting victims.

And so now I write both science fiction and vampire horror stories because I still can't control my active imagination. I hope you enjoy my humble offerings. You can reach me at SylyntStorme@gmail.com.

Visit me at www.SylyntStorme.com to stay up to date on new stories as they come out.

OTHER BOOKS BY SYLYNT STORME

Sylynt Storme currently writes both science fiction and horror stories. The Misgivings of the Vampire Lucius Lafayette series of which this book is a part is vampire fiction. But unlike any vampires you might have read about.

This book you've finished reading is The Vampire Lucius Lafayette: Volume 2 and contains the stories of The Misgivings of the Vampires Lucius Lafayette series numbered 5, 6, 7 and 8. All The Misgivings of the Vampire Lucius Lafayette stories can be bought individually. You can also buy The Misgivings of the Vampire Lucius Lafayette stories numbered 1, 2, 3 and 4 as a four pack. The Vampire Lucius Lafayette: Volume 1 contains stories numbered 1, 2, 3 and 4.

Here are the complete series of The Misgivings of the Vampire Lucius Lafayette stories written to date. Please visit www.SylyntStorme.com for new stories as this is an ongoing series:

1. Leather Apron
2. Mardi Gras
3. Hemlock Crescent
4. Hell's Disciples
5. Death's Door
6. Caged Heart
7. Broken Heart
8. Warmongers

Additionally, Sylynt Storme writes science fiction stories, or more specifically, space opera stories under the series called Star Sails. Please visit www.SylyntStorme.com for more information on where to buy any of the collections or individual short stories for all e-readers. Additionally, the compilations are available in paper as well.